"Why the sudden interest in *my* marriage, Garrett?"

In response he shrugged—then grasped her arms, pulling her down beside him. "Women who have *been* married don't usually shy away from physical contact the way you do."

"Meaning I'm supposed to be hungry for any man, even you?" Her eyes flashed before losing their fire. "Why don't you just leave me alone! I don't want you to touch me. I don't want—"

"Sarah...I have to touch you." His mouth was descending to hers. "I want you, Sarah, and I think you want me."

"No—" Tears scalded her cheeks. This was wrong, so very wrong. She hated this man, despised him. But she was returning his passion as if her very life depended on it.

This was the reason she hated Garrett, the reason her own marriage had never stood a chance, because it was Garrett she loved—had always loved.

CAROLE MORTIMER, one of our most popular—and prolific—English authors, began writing in the Harlequin Presents series in 1979. She now has more than forty top-selling romances to her credit and shows no signs whatever of running out of plot ideas. She writes strong traditional romances with a distinctly modern appeal, and her winning way with characters and romantic plot twists has earned her an enthusiastic audience worldwide.

Books by Carole Mortimer

HARLEQUIN PRESENTS

HARLEQUIN SIGNATURE EDITION

Don't miss any of our special offers. Write to us at the following address for information on our newest releases.

Harlequin Reader Service
901 Fuhrmann Blvd., P.O. Box 1397, Buffalo, NY 14240
Canadian address: P.O. Box 603,
Fort Erie, Ont. L2A 5X3

CAROLE MORTIMER

tangled hearts

Harlequin Books

TORONTO • NEW YORK • LONDON
AMSTERDAM • PARIS • SYDNEY • HAMBURG
STOCKHOLM • ATHENS • TOKYO • MILAN

For John
Matthew and Joshua

Harlequin Presents first edition December 1987
ISBN 0-373-11037-5

Original hardcover edition published in 1987
by Mills & Boon Limited

CHAPTER ONE

'ARE you my mother . . .?'

Sarah looked up from the half-completed canvas of the sea before her, her polite denial never uttered as she looked up at the pale youth beside her. He looked about fifteen or sixteen, wearing faded denims and a tight T-shirt, a faded denim jacket thrown over one shoulder in the heat of the day and held there by one finger. Thick blond hair grew almost down to his shoulders, streaked with white where he seemed to have spent hours in the sun. And green eyes, he had green eyes; Garrett Kingham's eyes.

The last time she had seen Jason, for this surely had to be him, he had been five years old, a boy with troubled green eyes, having been deeply disturbed by the discord between his parents. He had become a handsome youth, still a little gangly, but she had no doubt the lean, tall body would fill out during the next few years and he would be as muscular as his father.

Garrett Kingham. She could still remember the look on his face the last time she had seen him, the disgust expressed there as she ran at him kicking and screaming, punching futilely against his broad chest at his decision to take Jason away with him.

And now Jason had come back. She could hardly believe it!

'Sorry.' The youth gave a self-conscious grimace, suddenly looking very young. 'You couldn't be my mother, she's dead, and you're far too young to be *my* mother. I——It was just that you looked like I remember her,' he added sheepishly.

'Jason——'

'You know my name!' His eyes narrowed suspiciously. 'Who are you?'

Sarah put down her brush, picking up a paint-spattered cloth to wipe her hands. 'Who did you come here to see?' she prompted gently.

'My grandfather and—you have to be my Aunt Sarah,' he realised in some relief. 'For a moment I thought I was seeing a ghost.'

Amanda would be a ten-year-old ghost by now. For that was how long her sister had been dead. In fact, the similarity between herself and Amanda was only superficial; both had thick black hair, deep blue eyes, and small slender bodies, but their features could only be called vaguely similar. But Jason had only been five when his mother died, and possibly the similarity between the sisters now seemed more than it actually had been.

She gave her nephew a dazzling smile, standing up. 'Yes, I'm your Aunt Sarah,' she confirmed brightly. 'Have you been up to the cottage yet? Your grandfather is going to be pleased to see you.'

Jason shook his head, looking a little nervous now. 'There's no one there.'

'He said something earlier about walking into the village for his tobacco,' she dismissed lightly. 'Why didn't you let us know you were coming? Does your father know you're here?' she added warily; Garrett Kingham had never been particularly fond of his wife's family, and she had no reason to suppose that had changed over the years.

Jason didn't answer, his hands thrust into the back pockets of his denims as he turned to look out at the sea. 'Can you surf here?' He frowned at the gently falling waves against the sand.

'No,' she laughed regretfully. 'Although we do have windsurfing.'

He nodded, turning back to her. 'Is it always this windy here?' he asked ruefully.

'The east coast of England is known for it,' she acknowledged with a grimace. 'Jason——'

'Do you think my grandfather is back yet?' he cut in firmly. 'I'd really like to see him.'

'He'll want to see you too.' She quickly packed away her things. 'But you have to tell me whether or not your father knows you've come here,' she persisted.

A mutinous expression marred his youthful good looks. 'I'm sixteen——'

'Not until next month,' Sarah reminded him gently, very much afraid Garrett Kingham had no idea where his son was. And from what she remembered of him he wouldn't take lightly the news of Jason being here.

'I'm old enough to make my own decisions,' insisted Jason stubbornly.

She would be very interested to know what decision he had made that had brought him here, but now didn't seem the time to ask him, his manner being defensive to say the least.

Sarah's initial instinct had been to hug him, but he was at an age where such a show of emotion would only embarrass him. And so she continued to act calmly, as if it was perfectly normal for the nephew she hadn't seen for ten years to arrive so unexpectedly.

'Could you carry this for me?' She held out her canvas. 'Careful,' she warned. 'It's still wet.'

'Hey, this is good,' Jason admired in some surprise. 'Are you an artist?'

'No,' she denied, tucking her easel and chair under her arm, smiling her thanks as Jason bent to pick up her box of oil paints. 'I'm not the struggling-in-the-garret type,' she derided. 'No pun intended!' she added drily. 'I'm an art teacher during term time, I only "struggle" during the holidays!'

Jason gave a wary frown. 'You don't *look* like a schoolteacher.'

Sarah was familiar with this reaction from children of Jason's age; schoolteachers represented an authority they were beginning to resent. 'School teachers aren't wearing denim cut-offs and bikini-tops in America?' she teased.

'Not in class, anyway,' he drawled.

'Neither would I,' she mocked, as the two of them walked side by side across the beach towards her home that overlooked the sea. It was more of a cottage than a house, with three small bedrooms and a bathroom above the sitting-room and kitchen. She knew that Jason and his father lived in a house in Malibu, for she had excitedly read Amanda's glowing description of the house and swimming-pool when her sister first moved in there with Garrett Kingham over sixteen years ago, and it had sounded like a wonderful place to the impressionable ten-year-old she had been then. She was sure the cottage would seem very small to Jason in comparison; Amanda had certainly been dismayed by the smallness of it on the few occasions she had come home for a visit after her marriage. But it had been Sarah's home all her life, and she loved it.

'It isn't just the way you're dressed.' Jason still frowned. 'You don't look old enough to be a teacher.'

She gave him a teasing look. 'I've never yet been mistaken for one of my pupils!' She pushed open the cottage door, stacking all her equipment in a tiny room off the hallway. 'Have you eaten or can I get you something now?' She looked at her nephew expectantly.

'I've eaten,' he shruggingly refused, looking around him interestedly. 'Thank you,' he added awkwardly as she continued to look at him. 'Maybe you are a teacher after all,' he said ruefully.

'Maybe I am,' she nodded, eyes twinkling deeply blue. 'How about a drink?'

'Coke?'

'If that's what you'd like.' She led the way to the kitchen at the side of the cottage, the outside wall of the room dominated by a large window so that the beach and sea were still visible. 'Sit down.' She indicated the bar-stools that were tucked tidily under the breakfast bar in front of the window. 'Have you come far?' she asked conversationally as she opened the refrigerator door.

He smiled, suddenly looking boyish instead of the man he had been trying to appear since his arrival. 'You're persistent, aren't you?' He took the can of Coke, ignoring the glass, sipping thirstily from the can.

'And you're evasive,' Sarah frowned.

'Do you think my grandfather will be much longer?' he asked curiously.

If he had been one of her pupils evading an answer in this way she would have known how to handle him, but he was the nephew she hadn't seen for ten years, and she was so pleased to have him here that she didn't want him to leave again because she had probed too deeply too fast. No doubt he would tell them what he wanted to, in time. But one thing she was already sure of: his father didn't know where he was, and knowing Garrett Kingham as she did she knew he was sure to be furious when he found out Jason had come to them.

'I'm sure he'll be home any minute now,' she assured Jason, surprised that her father wasn't already back. 'Now——' She broke off as the front door slammed shut. 'That will be him now.' She smiled encouragingly at Jason as he suddenly looked nervous.

'I thought you would still be down on the beach, Sarah,' her father greeted her smilingly. He was short like her, his black hair liberally sprinkled with grey, his eyes a warm, twinkling blue. 'I walked down to join you when I got back from——' He came to a halt in the doorway as he saw she wasn't alone, his eyes widening with anticipation as he got a good look at their visitor. 'Jason?' he said half eagerly, half disbelievingly.

Jason had stood up slowly at his grandfather's entrance, and now he wiped his hands nervously down the sides of his denims. 'Grandad,' he nodded abruptly, swallowing hard.

Sarah felt an emotional lump catch in her throat at the way her father's face lit up at the sight of his only grandchild. He had talked a lot about Jason, since he had had more time to sit and brood over the past after his retirement a year ago, and she knew how much he had missed seeing his grandchild grow up, doing all the things with him a grandfather liked to do. If only she had had children, maybe he wouldn't have felt Jason's loss so deeply— no, she wouldn't dwell on what hadn't been, like her father; she would enjoy the fact that they had Jason with them now.

'Don't grandads get a hug in America?' her father teased Jason, who was waiting expectantly.

The boy moved awkwardly into his grandfather's arms, taller than the older man by several inches, even at only fifteen. He was going to be as tall as his father one day—— Sarah's delight faded a little as she acknowledged she was going to have to let Garrett Kingham know where his son was. And as soon as she did that, he would come and take Jason away from them again.

'——and so I thought you must have changed your mind,' she heard her father say fondly.

Sarah eyed the two suspiciously as they stood apart now. 'Changed his mind about what?' she frowned.

'Er—how about a cup of tea, Sarah, love?' her father evaded.

'Dad!' She looked at him sternly, sure now that the two of them had been up to something she knew nothing about.

'Let's not argue in front of Jason when he's come to see us after all these years——'

'Dad, you——'

'It's like this, Aunt Sarah,' Jason cut in, in a self-possessed voice that sounded too old for his almost sixteen years. 'I telephoned Grandad yesterday and asked him if I could come visit the two of you.'

Now that Sarah gave it some thought she supposed she had noticed an air of excitement about her father since she got in from shopping yesterday afternoon, but she had imagined that to be because Mrs Potter from the village had called in to spend a few hours with him while she was out. Her father and Glynis Potter had been seeing a lot of each other over the last few months, and because she knew her father felt embarrassed about having a 'girl-friend' at his age she hadn't ever mentioned that she knew about the two of them. Now it seemed her father had been keeping something much more serious than his friendship with Glynis from her!

'Why didn't you tell me?' She sighed her disappointment in him.

'Now don't upset yourself, Sarah,' he soothed. 'I couldn't be sure Jason would really come here, and I—I didn't want to disappoint you if he couldn't make it after all.'

Her expression softened as she guessed *he* would have been the one unable to bear the disappointment if they had made preparations and then Jason hadn't arrived. She could see it in his eyes now as he looked at Jason, knew he hadn't been able to put it into words that Jason might visit because until he had seen Jason sitting in the kitchen waiting for him to come home, it had all seemed as if it might just be a dream.

'Okay, you two conspirators,' she teased. 'What was the plan?'

'You see,' her father grinned at Jason, 'didn't I tell you she's a good sport!'

She didn't feel much like a 'good sport', not when she knew Garrett Kingham was going to be furious when he found out they had known since yesterday of Jason's visit and hadn't chosen to inform him. Oh, *she* hadn't technically known about it, but she knew Garrett Kingham was never going to believe that.

'I'll make the tea,' her father offered brightly now that the moment of danger had passed. 'You two go and sit down in the other room.'

Their sitting-room also doubled as the room where her father designed and built models of old sailing ships, as her sewing-room, and sometimes as an art studio. Nevertheless it was clean and comfortable, and Sarah only had to move a couple of books from chairs to make room for them all to sit down.

Jason seemed more relaxed too now. 'He's just as I imagined he would be,' he grinned.

Had Garrett Kingham ever looked as boyish as his son did now? she wondered. She doubted it. The younger son of Senator Kingham—the elder son Jonathan having followed in the career of his father and also become a senator in recent years—Garrett Kingham had been born with a golden spoon in his mouth, had gone to all the best schools, and then to the world-famous Harvard, before deciding to make a career for himself as a film director. He had fought family opposition, the prejudice towards him from others in the profession, to become one of the most ruthlessly successful directors Hollywood had ever known. And he hadn't done any of it by being nice, let alone boyish!

Garrett Kingham had been twenty-three when Amanda had brought him home as her husband, but to the ten-year-old Sarah he had already seemed old, had already clawed his way half-way up the ladder of success, the hardness of his eyes letting everyone know that he clearly intended to make it the rest of the way up, no matter who got in his way. His marriage to Amanda had been one of the things that got in his way.

Her sister, much against her parents' wishes, had gone off to Hollywood at the age of eighteen to 'find success and happiness'. Six months later she had arrived home as Garrett Kingham's bride and expecting his baby!

Sarah had watched as her parents did their best to welcome the worldly, cynical young man into their family, and Amanda had seemed happy enough with the way things had worked out, but Sarah couldn't hide the fact that she didn't like her new brother-in-law one bit. He had seemed to be looking down his aristocratic nose at them all the time, even insisting he and Amanda stay at a local hotel when there was a perfectly good third bedroom at the cottage that they could have used, that had always been Amanda's room. Not that Garrett had seemed in the least concerned with the obvious dislike of a ten-year-old; he had ignored her where he possibly could.

No, even though Garrett had only been eight years older than Jason was now when she first met him, Sarah knew he had never been boyish, had probably never been young at all!

'We've thought of you often over the years,' she told Jason huskily.

'You never missed a single birthday,' he acknowledged gruffly. 'Or Christmas.'

Although Garrett Kingham had never encouraged their interest in Jason after he took him away, they hadn't thought he could possibly object to the small gifts they sent Jason on his birthday and at Christmas. The gifts were never returned, and several weeks later they would always receive a thank you letter from Jason. It had been the only contact they had had with him over the years.

'Here we are.' Her father came in with the tray of tea. 'I brought you another Coke, Jason,' he told him, sitting down to gaze at the boy fondly as Sarah poured the tea. 'I always knew you would look like your father,' he said ruefully. 'Even as a baby you had none of the Harvey colouring.'

Jason's expression was suddenly guarded, as if he sensed criticism.

'I think it's as well he inherited Garrett's height,' Sarah put in lightly, anxious to reassure Jason that her father hadn't meant anything by his observation. 'We Harveys aren't known for our stature!' She mocked her father's and her own lack of inches, relieved when Jason gave a relaxed grin. 'You never did tell me what plans the two of you had made for meeting today?' she reintroduced casually.

Jason shrugged. 'Dad's in England making a film, and I thought it would be nice to come see the two of you.'

Garrett Kingham was actually in England! Sarah's hands clenched in reaction to that piece of information. Ten years ago she had no longer been a child, and yet she had flown at Garrett Kingham like a wild thing; she hadn't seen him since that fateful day. And she didn't want to see him again now, although surely with Jason here that was inevitable.

'He brought you over with him for a holiday?' she asked interestedly.

'Because he had to,' Jason corrected harshly. 'Unfortunately for him he couldn't dump me on Uncle Jonathan and Aunt Shelley like he usually does because they're away themselves at the moment.'

There was a wealth of bitterness in the words, and Sarah wondered just how often Jason had been 'dumped' on his aunt and uncle over the years. Too many times, by the sound of it.

Ten years ago Garrett had made it clear that any effort they made to see his son would be rebuffed, and for Jason's sake, because they didn't think it fair to place that sort of burden on such a young child, they had respected that decision, no matter how much it had hurt them to do so. Now that Jason was old enough to make his own decisions about such things it seemed he felt differently about his grandfather and aunt. She was glad, although she knew Garrett wouldn't be.

'I'm sure he doesn't just "dump" you, Jason,' she reproved gently. 'He has to work, after all.

And I'm sure your aunt and uncle are very nice.'

'They're okay,' he dismissed. 'But Dad doesn't *have* to work; he has enough money not to.'

'Don't you think thirty-nine is a little young to retire?' she chided.

Anger flared in the brilliant green eyes, and Sarah could see that the last thing Jason had expected was that she would actually defend his father over this. But she wasn't taking anyone's side, was just trying to show Jason that there were always two sides to everything. Secretly she thought it was a good thing that Garrett had been forced to bring his son with him this time, and not just because it gave them the opportunity to spend some time with Jason; it sounded to her as if the two of *them* spent too little time together even when Garrett was at home.

'He——'

'I'm sorry I missed your bus arriving, Jason,' his grandfather cut in with a warning glance at Sarah. 'Usually it's late, and I thought I had left home in plenty of time to meet you off it, only to find when I got to the village that today of all days it had been early!'

So that was why her father had decided to go down to the village mid-week for his tobacco; usually he took a walk down on a Saturday! 'I gather the two of you missed each other,' she said drily.

'Mm,' her father grimaced. 'By the time I reached the village the bus had long gone, and Mrs Hall at the shop didn't know if a young man had got off it or not. I thought perhaps Jason had changed his mind and not come after all.'

Once again her throat filled emotionally at the way her father looked at his grandson. Her father had always been a wonderful parent, had always had time and love for her and Amanda, and he should have had half a dozen grandchildren he could spoil by now. But Amanda had only had Jason and she—her pupils were *her* children!

'I asked directions to the cottage at the gas station,' Jason explained. 'They said it would be quicker if I followed the coast round, so I walked along the beach.'

'It is quicker that way,' his grandfather nodded. 'But all that sand makes my old legs ache!'

'Don't pay any attention to him, Jason,' Sarah derided. 'He's been telling me how old he is for the last twenty years!'

'And she's never let me get away with it,' her father grimaced. 'Believe me, after living in a houseful of women all these years it's nice to have another male in residence for a while.'

Sarah's eyes widened as she looked at the two of them. 'Jason intends staying with us?' A day visit was one thing, but she didn't think Garrett Kingham would allow anything else.

'If that's all right with you.' Jason was at once on the defensive.

'Of course. I just——'

'The spare room is always ready for guests,' his grandfather assured him jovially. 'Did you bring any clothes with you?'

Jason nodded, still watching Sarah warily. 'I left my back-pack outside,' he answered slowly.

The last thing she wanted to appear was the spoiler of all their fun, but even so . . . 'Does your father know where you are?' she asked with firm control, demanding an answer this time.

Jason flushed. 'He's away in Scotland for a couple of days with the owner of the studio. I was sick of sitting around in a hotel room, so I gave Grandad a call.'

'But even so——'

'Jason, why don't you go and get your things and take them upstairs,' his grandfather suggested lightly. 'It's the room on the right at the top of the stairs.'

Jason looked about to argue, and then he nodded reluctant agreement, his mouth set rebelliously as he went outside.

'I know you're angry, Sarah,' her father soothed before she could speak. 'But when he called me yesterday the lad was upset; what else could I do but invite him to come here?'

'You know I don't mind the fact that he's here,' she admonished. 'I'm as pleased to see him as you are. I just think you should have acted a little more responsibly and——'

'How could I tell Garrett when he isn't even at the hotel?' he reasoned.

'You could have left a message for him,' she pointed out gently.

'All right,' her father admitted irritably. 'I'll admit that I was so excited at the thought of seeing Jason again after all these years that I may have acted a little selfishly. But it isn't too late to leave a message at the hotel for Garrett now; Jason said he isn't due back for a couple more days. I didn't see why the lad should be bored waiting for him at that hotel when he could be with us,' he added persuasively.

Her father was worse than Jason, and despite his sixty-six years he seemed about the same age at the moment, excited at the prospect of having Jason stay with them, if only for a few days. Sarah doubted if either of them would listen if she pointed out that it was probably because all Jason would have to do if Garrett brought him with him was sit bored around hotels, that Garrett thought it best if he stayed with his aunt and uncle at these times! Not that she thought Garrett was right completely; heaven forbid she should think that man was right about anything! But he was Jason's father, and he was going to be worried about him once he learnt of his disappearance.

She stood up decisively as Jason came back into the room, eyeing them both suspiciously. 'Don't look so worried, Jason,' she said lightly. 'All we've decided is to leave a message at the hotel for your father telling him where you are.'

She made no comment as he mumbled the name of one of the most prestigious hotels in London; where else would Garrett Kingham stay, the famous film director, son and brother to Washington senators!

As soon as she got through to the hotel and asked to leave a message for Mr Kingham there was a strange clicking noise on the line and then a very short ring before the receiver was picked up the other end. 'Hello, I——'

'Who is this?' demanded a gravelly voice that was definitely American-accented.

But not Garrett's voice, thank goodness! 'I

wanted to leave a message for Mr Kingham,' she said awkwardly, completely disconcerted, having expected to speak to the receptionist. 'But there seems to have been some sort of confusion, because the operator——'

'What's the message?' that gravelly voice demanded again, and Sarah instantly formed an image of a six-and-a-half-foot giant with the build of Arnold Schwarzenegger—but without the intelligence that man had displayed when she had seen him on a chat show several months ago!

'If you gave me a chance to finish speaking I would tell you,' she said in her sternest school-teacher voice, receiving silent attention for her effort. 'Could you please tell Mr Kingham that Sarah rang, and that——'

'Sarah who?'

This conversation wasn't going at all as smoothly as she had hoped, and she was glad she was out in the hallway and didn't have an audience to her embarrassment. The man on the other end of the telephone line had the finesse of a bull-dozer! Although he probably had a point: Garrett Kingham probably knew a hundred women named Sarah—all of them intimately.

'Sarah——' She hesitated. If she said Sarah Croft then Garrett probably wouldn't realise who she was; she doubted he had troubled himself to learn that his once-sister-in-law had been married and divorced since they had last met. 'Sarah Harvey,' she decided firmly. 'Could you tell him Jason is with us, and that——'

'You've got the kid?' The gravelly voice was instantly alert, making Sarah wonder if she could

possibly have underestimated his intelligence just
because she didn't like the sound of his voice.

She bristled indignantly. 'His name is Jason.
And yes, he's with us. I wanted to——'

'*What* do you want?' the man growled.

Sarah gave a start at the aggression. 'If you
would just let me finish speaking instead of——'

'I think I should warn you that you aren't being
clever, that the kid's old man is angry, very angry,
so if you——'

'No more angry than I am, let me assure you,'
she snapped furiously. 'Now would you kindly tell
Mr Kingham that Jason is with us, and that if he
wants him he's going to have to come here and get
him!' She slammed the receiver down, glaring at
it indignantly, as if it were its fault she had just
been spoken to so rudely. She was shaking because
she was so angry, had never been spoken to in that
aggressively rude way before.

Jason looked up at her searchingly as she went
back into the lounge with controlled violence,
pacing the room, still too angry to sit down. 'What
happened?' he finally asked wearily.

Her eyes blazed with fiery blue sparks as she
turned to face him. 'I've just spoken to the rudest
man——'

'Dad?' He looked anxious. 'But he isn't supposed to be back——'

'It certainly wasn't your father,' she snapped.
'If it had been I would have known how to deal
with him. This man sounded like an all-in-
wrestler and heavy-weight boxer rolled into
one——'

'Dennis,' Jason said knowingly.

'*Dennis*?' she repeated incredulously, trying to see the owner of that voice answering to such a name—and failing. Killer, sounded more appropriate! But he must have been a baby once; how could his mother be expected to know he would grow up to resemble a gorilla?

'What did he say to you?' Jason's eyes were narrowed questioningly.

She was about to launch into a word-for-word account of the conversation when she remembered what Dennis had said about Garrett being very angry concerning Jason's disappearance. She had no idea when Garrett was going to come for his son, and she didn't see why Jason should be in a state of apprehension until he did deign to do so.

'I just didn't like his manner,' she avoided. 'But he said he would let your father know you're staying with us.'

Jason frowned. 'He didn't say anything else?'

She gave a rueful smile. 'I'm afraid I didn't give him chance to; I slammed the phone down!'

Jason raised amused brows. 'I bet Dennis just loved that!'

'I really couldn't give a—care less about what Dennis loves,' she dismissed. 'Now, how about the two of you helping me get a meal ready, and then we can all sit down and have a chat?'

They had fun all crowded together in the kitchen, tripping over each other most of the time. Jason was a little uncertain what to do at first, which reminded Sarah that he probably didn't do any of these things for himself at home, that Garrett Kingham probably had a houseful of servants to do things for them. Jason seemed to find it all the more fun because of that.

It was an enjoyable meal, her father in his element with his grandson there, the two of them managing to draw out more information about Jason's life with his father without being too obvious about it. He certainly didn't sound like an underprivileged child, but his visit here today meant he obviously felt something was missing from his life. Sarah only hoped Garrett Kingham realised that was his reason for coming here before venting his 'anger' on anyone.

If Jason found their cottage cramped after the spacious luxury he was used to he didn't show it, and was already sleeping like a baby by the time Sarah checked on him on the way to her own bed. Her father had gone up to his room at the same time Jason had, mainly, Sarah was sure, because he didn't want any more lectures on how irresponsible his behaviour had been concerning Jason. Jason had acted impetuously, but her father had known better than to agree without first consulting Garrett, and he knew it; Sarah considered she had said enough on the subject to make him realise that.

She smiled indulgently as she prepared for bed. Her father really was incorrigible! He—— She fastened her robe over her cotton pyjamas as she heard the sound of a car stopping outside; it was almost midnight!

It was a clear night, and silhouetted against the moonlight was the tall figure of a man with silver-blond hair. Garrett Kingham ...

CHAPTER TWO

WELL, she had told Dennis to tell him that if he wanted Jason he was going to have to come and get him, Sarah thought ruefully as she hurried down the stairs to answer his thunderous knocking on the door before he woke her father and Jason up too; she just hadn't expected him to get here this quickly!

She unlocked the door, barely having time to pull back the bolt at the top before the door was pushed open and Garrett Kingham strode inside without giving her so much as a second glance; the first one had been enough, ripping into her! He certainly hadn't changed, she acknowledged as she closed the door behind him and followed him through to the sitting-room.

He was so tall he made the room seem smaller than ever, his silver-blond hair brushing against the ceiling, the width of his shoulders completely blocking her view of the painting that stood over the fireplace behind him. Green eyes narrowed as he looked at her coldly, his nostrils flared, his mouth tight. And it was still the most handsome face Sarah had ever seen, powerful and magnetic, his muscled body exuding the same power in the black shirt and black fitted denims.

As he silently continued to look at her Sarah

began to shift uncomfortably. Her knee-length
cotton robe matched the blue pyjamas she wore
beneath it, her hair was soft and silky after its
nightly brushing. She felt sixteen again, and she
knew she probably looked it!

'As instructed,' he finally bit out. 'I've come for
my son.'

Like icy fragments his voice cut into her. She
drew herself up to her full height of five feet two
inches. 'Jason is asleep upstairs,' she informed him
haughtily. 'Maybe if you had arrived at a
respectable time instead of——'

'I had to fly down from Scotland before coming
the rest of the way by car,' he rasped.

'Oh yes,' she taunted. 'You left Jason alone in
London while you went away on business.'

Garrett's gaze didn't falter, not a muscle moved
in his face, and yet the anger emanating from him
now seemed more intense. 'Jason wasn't alone,' he
told her coldly.

'Oh no, of course he wasn't, he had Dennis with
him,' she scorned. 'He must be a delightful
companion for a fifteen-year-old boy!'

'Jason is hardly a boy any longer,' Garrett bit
out stiffly. 'And Dennis isn't supposed to be his
companion!'

Looking at him now, Sarah could easily see how
Amanda had initially fallen in love with this man.
It also wasn't difficult to see why he had made
Amanda so unhappy after their marriage; he had
the surface attraction to entice any woman, it was

only on the inside that he was cold and empty, unable to love.

'Nevertheless, you left Jason alone with him in a hotel in London——'

'Not that I have to explain my actions to you,' Garrett looked at her coldly, 'but I asked Jason to go up to Scotland with me, and he declined in favour of sightseeing in London.'

Sarah gave a perplexed frown. She doubted Garrett felt the need to lie about his motives to her, which meant that Jason had—— But no, he hadn't actually said his father had left him in London either, only that he was sick of sitting in a hotel room; she had just assumed—— Maybe in future, with her dislike of Garrett so intense, it would be better if she didn't *assume* anything about him.

'I must have misunderstood him,' she avoided awkwardly. 'But that still doesn't excuse the fact that you left him with that——'

'I left him with his bodyguard,' Garrett cut in arrogantly. 'As I always do when I'm unable to be with him myself.'

'Bodyguard?' Sarah repeated shakily, suddenly pale. 'Why on earth would Jason need a bodyguard?'

Garrett's mouth twisted. 'Because he comes from a rich family——'

'A rich and *powerful* family,' she amended flatly.

'And powerful,' he acknowledged with an inclination of his head. 'And because kidnapping the children of the rich and powerful for ransom seems to be in fashion in the States at the moment.'

Sarah swallowed hard. 'Then when I telephoned earlier Dennis must have thought, you must all have thought——'

'That Jason had been kidnapped and you were telephoning with the ransom demand, yes,' Garrett confirmed grimly. 'It was all I could do to prevent Dennis from coming here with me once he had relayed your message to me and I told him I knew where Jason was; he thought you were trying to lure *me* into a trap,' he derided.

The thought of some six-and-a-half-foot muscle-man demanding entrance to her home made her feel ill.

'But I assured him you were only my sister-in-law,' Garrett taunted at her sickly pallor. 'And that Jason had decided to pay you an unscheduled visit.'

Her eyes flashed angrily, a flush to her cheeks now. 'How could a visit to us from Jason be anything but unscheduled?'

His mouth thinned. 'Jason has never shown the slightest inclination before to visit you and your father.'

'Well, obviously he now feels differently about that,' she snapped, unable to subdue the antagonism she always felt around this man.

'Without asking my permission,' his father rasped harshly.

'Does he have to ask your permission for everything he does?' she challenged.

Green eyes ripped into her coldly. 'Jason is still only fifteen years old, and I think taking off on a whim is a little more serious than asking to go to the damned bathroom!'

He was right, of course he was right, Jason should never have just left the way he had and worried everyone. But it was the way Garrett called Jason visiting her father and her a 'whim' that rankled! 'I realise he shouldn't have done this quite the way that he did, but I also——'

'How magnanimous of you,' Garrett drawled.

She flashed him a look of intense dislike. 'But maybe if he felt close enough to you to be able to talk to you he could have told you how curious he felt about us!' she snapped.

Garrett drew in a harsh breath, his expression contemptuous. 'On the basis of a few hours' acquaintance with Jason you have decided that I'm a totally unfit father who at best ignores him, and at worst browbeats him?'

'No, of course not——'

'It certainly sounds like it to me!'

'It wasn't just that——'

'No, I forgot,' he rasped. 'There's also the fact that you already disliked me intensely and would gladly believe anything anyone said against me!'

It had never been difficult to hate this man, it was true, to hate the way he had preferred Amanda not to visit her family after they were married, the pain he had caused Amanda during their marriage, until it became so impossible for her to live with a man who didn't love her that she had finally left him and come home, only to be killed in a motorway pile-up the day after her arrival back in England. Garrett Kingham had arrived in time for Amanda's funeral, and after the service he had told them he was taking Jason back to the States with him. The five-year-old boy was all they had left of Amanda, and Sarah could see how it was breaking her father's heart to part with him too. But Garrett was immune to their pleadings, until finally, impatiently, Sarah had flown at him, screaming and kicking as she told him how much she hated him.

She had been sixteen then, her body mature but her emotions still those of a child, and all she had been able to think of was that he had hurt her sister and that he was taking Jason away from them too. She was a woman now, but she still hated him.

She looked at him coldly. 'Maybe that's because it's always so easy *to* believe!'

He sighed. 'Sarah, it's late, I've had a long journey to get here, and I'm in no mood to argue with you.'

She stood firm in spite of the lines of tiredness she could now see beside his eyes and mouth. She didn't want to think of this man as vulnerable, because that would make him human, and she knew that was something he wasn't. 'I told you, Jason is asleep, and, unlike the last time you dragged Jason out of his bed and away from us, I am now all grown-up and more than capable of handling you without resorting to violence!'

She wished she had never issued the challenge

as his narrowed gaze moved over her insolently in a totally male assessment, making her instantly aware of her own inadequacies. She didn't need Garrett Kingham's contempt to tell her that although she was slender enough her body certainly wasn't of the shape to drive a man wild with desire, just as she also didn't need him to tell her that, although she and Amanda had a surface similarity, Amanda was the one that had sparkled and charmed, while she just quietly glowed.

Garrett's mouth quirked in the semblance of a smile. 'You don't look any different to me now than you did at sixteen,' he taunted. 'Or any more capable of "handling" me.'

'No?' she flared at his condescension. 'Then perhaps you would like to try and take Jason away again?'

His eyes narrowed to icy emerald slits. 'I don't like being threatened, Sarah.'

'Really?' she challenged, her head back. 'Well, neither do I!'

They continued to glare at each other for several tension-filled minutes, Sarah determined not to be the one who backed down—mainly because she had no idea *how* to stop him taking Jason away now if he wanted to do so, despite her claim to the contrary. All she knew was that Jason was no longer a child to be dragged away when he didn't want to go, and that it would break her father's heart a second time if by some miracle Garrett persuaded Jason to go with him now. Her mother had died twelve years go, Amanda ten years ago, and she and Jason were all her father had left. She *would* keep Jason here, if only until tomorrow when he could say goodbye to them properly.

Finally Garrett was the one to drop his gaze, sighing as he folded his length down into one of the fireside armchairs. 'Do you still make a delicious cup of coffee?' he asked wearily.

She blinked. 'I still make the *same* coffee.' She wasn't even prepared to take a compliment about such a trivial thing from this man!

He nodded. 'Strong, just the way I like it. Black, please.'

She wanted to tell him that it was after twelve o'clock at night, that she was tired too, and certainly not in the mood to make coffee for anyone. But despite herself she could see that he really *was* tired, looking all of his thirty-nine years as he relaxed back in the chair. And with that realisation came the knowledge that he must have been worried out of his mind about Jason before receiving her call, that whatever else she thought about him, he did seem to love his son.

On the few occasions she had allowed herself to dwell on the past, Garrett had always seemed ageless to her, but now she could see that the years hadn't dealt kindly with him, that his hair wasn't blond at his temples but grey, giving it a salt-and-pepper look, the deep lines of cynicism beside his mouth long ago having banished any claim he might have had to youth. If he had made those around him unhappy he certainly hadn't fared any better himself.

'Very well, Mr Kingham,' she sighed. 'Then I would suggest you——'

'My name is Garrett, Sarah, as you very well know,' he said drily. 'Prove you aren't still a child and use it.'

Her cheeks were burning as she moved about the kitchen preparing the coffee. She was a teacher, had been a married woman, and yet something about Garrett Kingham reduced her to the petulant child she had always been in his presence. How could Amanda have ever fallen in love with such a man, despite his surface attraction?

Amanda had been beautiful all her life, could have had her pick of any of the local young men who always seemed to be at the cottage to see her, and yet she had wanted to go to America to become an actress, so sure that she would be a success, despite her parents' warning that every young girl who set out for Hollywood believed the same thing about herself, but few actually ever made it. Amanda had never actually appeared in a film, had become Garrett Kingham's wife instead, and apparently the Kingham wives didn't *work*. All Garrett required of her was that she be a mother to Jason and a beautiful hostess in his home. And Amanda had been good at both those things, had openly adored Jason, become *the* society hostess of Hollywood.

But even that success hadn't been enough for the arrogant Garrett Kingham, and for the most part he had ignored the existence of his wife and

son as he ruthlessly furthered his own career. He
had made Amanda miserable, and he couldn't be
allowed to continue doing the same to Jason,
Sarah decided determinedly.

Her expression was set aggressively as she
marched back into the sitting-room with the
coffee, only to have her determination completely
deflated as she saw that Garrett Kingham had
fallen asleep in the chair!

She put the tray down carefully, glaring at him
frustratedly. He looked only slightly younger in
sleep, as if even in that relaxed state he had to
maintain a guard over his emotions. Or maybe it
was as she had always suspected: he didn't have
any emotions that needed guarding!

No matter how tired he was he looked completely out of place in their comfortable sitting-
room, dominating even in sleep. And he couldn't
continue to sleep there, he had to leave.

'Garrett?' She shook his shoulder gently.
'Garrett, wake up!'

His answer was to fling her hand away from his
shoulder, his eyes hostile as he glared up at her.
'What the hell do you think you're doing?' he
grated harshly, straightening stiffly.

Sarah stuck her hand behind her back as if she
had been burnt. 'You fell asleep, and you can't
stay here,' she told him abruptly. 'I had no idea I
wasn't supposed to touch the great Garrett
Kingham!' she snapped scornfully.

Some of the tension left his body, determinedly
so, it seemed, his mouth twisting wryly. 'Believe

me,' he drawled, 'I'm not usually averse to having a beautiful woman touch me; you just startled me, that's all.'

She didn't want to hear about the women in his life, or his relationship with them. He had been her sister's husband, and as such she felt he should have kept his affairs to himself. 'I can assure you I won't do that again,' she bit out stiffly. 'I've brought your coffee. I suggest you drink it and then leave.'

He shook his head before drinking the black brew thirstily. 'Not without Jason,' he told her grimly.

Her cheeks were flushed. 'Jason said you're working in England at the moment; surely it isn't going to hurt anyone if he stays with us for a few days?' Her father had enjoyed being with his grandson so much this evening, and, while he knew Jason had to go back with his father some time, surely it didn't have to be just yet?

Garrett's expression was grim. 'Maybe if he had spoken to me about it——'

'You wouldn't have let him come here,' Sarah snapped. 'The same way you discouraged Amanda from visiting us once she was your wife.'

His eyes were narrowed, his expression cold. 'I never stopped Amanda from coming home.'

'I said discouraged,' she said sturdily. 'You made it pretty obvious you didn't approve of her coming here.'

'I—Sarah, let's not rehash history that's years old,' he sighed wearily. 'Jason knows better than to evade Dennis and just disappear the way that he did.'

It sounded very much as if he did, as if he had known exactly how much his actions would worry his father. 'In my experience his behaviour sounds like a cry for your attention——'

'And just how much experience of parenthood have you had, *Miss* Harvey?' he derided harshly.

Her cheeks were pale, her eyes stormy. 'I only told Dennis that my name was Sarah Harvey so that you would realise who was calling; my surname is actually Croft now,' she told him with dislike. 'And although I may not have any children of my own I am in charge of several hundred pupils during a day!'

His eyes were narrowed as he ignored the latter, staring at the bareness of her left hand. 'Are you telling me that you have a husband waiting for you upstairs?'

His incredulity angered her even further. 'Not any more, but I did, yes!'

Garrett's mouth twisted. 'The Harvey girls seem to make a habit of "running home to Daddy" when things don't go quite the way they want them to!' he said with derision.

'I didn't have to "run home", because David and I lived here with my father,' she blazed. 'And, for your information, David and I divorced amicably.' If her six months' marriage six years ago could be called that when it had been nothing but a disaster from start to finish!

'Maybe if he had been man enough to demand

that the two of you have your own home it wouldn't have happened!'

She wasn't about to tell this man that as a last resort she and David had even tried living on their own, that the marriage still hadn't worked. 'Don't presume to judge my marriage when you made such a mess of your own,' she scorned.

'Maybe if you and Amanda hadn't been spoilt by your parents all your lives you wouldn't throw a tantrum every time your husband failed to spoil you too!' he rasped harshly.

'Oh you—you——'

'Yes?' he mocked.

'Biased idiot!' she glared. 'Amanda and I were loved, not spoilt. It's obviously an emotion *your* family knows nothing about, you in particular!'

He rose slowly to his feet, instantly dwarfing her. 'There are many kinds of loving, Sarah,' he murmured softly. 'Which type did you have in mind?'

Her eyes were wide at the sudden threat he posed towards her. How had the conversation come around to *this*? 'I—no, Garrett.' She held up her hands defensively, only to have them flattened against his chest as his arms moved firmly about her. '*Garrett!*'

'Sarah,' he returned tauntingly, his expression grim. 'Whoever would have believed the little she-cat would grow up to be such a beautiful woman?' he mused before his head bent to hers.

His lips were cool and moist, and totally possessing as they claimed hers, and Sarah's last thought, before she couldn't think at all, was that this just couldn't be happening, not to her, and with *Garrett Kingham*.

And then her mind went completely blank as her body acknowledged the expertise of Garrett's mouth moving against hers, his hands roaming caressingly across her back and down to cup her bottom as he pulled her up against him. Sarah trembled as she felt the hardness of his body, gasping as she felt one of his hands move between them to unbutton her pyjama top.

His fingers were warm against her heated flesh as he undid first one button, then the second, and then the third, until her breasts were completely exposed and that hand moved confidently beneath the cotton material to cup and claim one of them.

His lips moved along the line of her jaw to tug on her exposed earlobe, before moving slowly down her throat to the breast that waited expectantly.

Sarah was trembling so badly that her knees shook, was feeling weak, and dizzy, and a hundred other emotions this man had no right to make her feel. Her eyes were squeezed tightly shut as his warmly sensuous mouth claimed her throbbing nipple, opening wide with dazed disbelief as he suddenly thrust her away from him. Had he just been playing with her, teaching her a lesson she would never forget? And she knew she never would forget!

'Cover yourself up,' he instructed harshly. 'Someone is coming down the stairs!'

The words were barely uttered when she too became aware of the sound of footsteps on the stairs, the heated colour leaving her cheeks as she hurriedly rebuttoned her pyjama top, Garrett stepping in front of her as the door opened, giving her the few precious seconds she needed to complete the task.

'Garrett!' her father greeted in some surprise. 'I had no idea . . . Sarah!' He gave a perplexed frown as she stepped out from behind Garrett.

She knew she must look flustered, although her pyjamas and robe were now refastened and tidily back in place. But her cheeks felt pale, and she knew her eyes were wide with the shock of what had just happened. And Garrett looked as coolly composed as ever.

'Garrett was—we were——'

'As you've probably guessed, I came to take Jason back to London with me,' Garrett cut in harshly. 'Sarah was just trying to persuade me to let him stay on with the two of you for a few days,' he added. 'I've told her I'll think about it. We certainly didn't mean to disturb you, Geoffrey,' he apologised abruptly.

Her father looked pleased at the fact that Garrett was actually considering letting Jason continue to stay with them, while Sarah felt sick at the implication behind Garrett's words. He seemed to think that she would willingly have given him her body in an effort to influence his decision in their favour!

She couldn't explain what had happened

between them just now. She realised for the first time that hate could be as powerful an inducement to passion as love. Because she hated Garrett Kingham more than she ever had!

Damn him and his biased presumptions!

'It doesn't matter,' her father dismissed, unaware of the friction between Garrett and Sarah. 'You don't need as much sleep when you're older.'

Garrett gave an abrupt inclination of his head. 'I'd better be on my way to the hotel. I'll be back in the morning,' he added warningly.

He was much quieter about leaving than he had been when he arrived, the car accelerating away seconds later.

'Well, what do you make of that?' her father mused in some surprise.

Sarah could see he was already anticipating that Garrett's answer to Jason staying on with them would be yes. She just didn't happen to have the same confidence. 'I think we'll have to see what he's decided in the morning,' she said resolutely.

'I would have asked him to stay, but——'

'Why leave yourself open to insult, Dad,' she dismissed, her eyes narrowed. 'Garrett Kingham is just as arrogant as he ever was!'

Her father shook his head sadly. 'I never could understand how Amanda became involved with him in the first place.'

Even Amanda hadn't seemed able to explain that, but on the day she married Garrett she had been three months pregnant with his child!

Her parents had been very upset when Amanda had introduced Garrett as her husband of a week, and in the same breath announced that they would be grandparents in six months' time. Sarah hadn't quite understood what all her mother's crying and her father's shaking of head was about, although she realised it had something to do with them not approving of Amanda's hasty marriage to Garrett Kingham. Sarah had been twelve before the full significance of Jason's birth so quickly after the wedding had become clear to her, and by that time her mother had died and her father become resigned to Amanda's marriage.

Her father sighed. 'When she left here she was so determined to become an actress; it came as a great surprise when she married Garrett and settled down to being a wife and mother!'

Sarah wouldn't have exactly called Amanda's parties and hectic social life 'settling down' to anything, but she understood what her father meant. 'Garrett has been successful enough for both of them,' she dismissed scathingly.

'Mm,' her father nodded with a sigh. 'But it hasn't made him happy.'

She wondered if Garrett had ever been happy. Not that she particularly cared; Garrett had disturbed her life enough during the last half-hour for her to hate him more than she already had.

'What do you think he'll decide about Jason?' her father frowned.

She was sure that Garrett had already decided to take Jason away with him in the morning, that he had only told her father he was thinking about letting him stay as a way of showing his contempt for her. After all, he was hardly likely to decide to leave his son in the care of a woman who had just shown him how wanton she could be. And with a man she had quite clearly shown she hated.

'Don't get your hopes up, Dad,' she advised him. 'I'm afraid my "persuasion" didn't influence him one little bit.'

Except maybe to convince him she wasn't a suitable companion for his son!

CHAPTER THREE

SARAH was dreading Garrett's arrival this morning, dreading having to face him again after what had happened between them the previous night. Not that she really knew what *had* happened! Oh, she could tell herself that they were both emotionally aroused, that she had been challenging his authority over Jason, she could even say that going down to talk to him in her nightclothes was an open invitation. What she *couldn't* say was why she had allowed a man she hated and despised to kiss her in that intimate way!

Her cheeks still burnt with the shame of it every time she remembered his mouth on her, those sensitively long hands against her creamy white breasts, his mouth—oh God, his mouth——! She couldn't stand to think of the places his mouth had roamed or the way she had been powerless to stop him!

How could she face him again knowing he had been perfectly aware of that?

Jason had greeted the news of his father's arrival the previous night with wary hostility, only picking at the breakfast Sarah had prepared for him, despite saying he was ravenous minutes earlier.

As she cleared away in the kitchen she could see

Jason and her father out on the beach now, engaging in a pebble-skimming contest, already seeming to know they would very shortly be saying goodbye. For her father's sake as well as Jason's she wished it didn't have to be so.

Everyone claimed that retirement was what you worked towards all your life, to the days when you didn't have to be a slave to your job any longer; they forgot to mention that without the job to go to there was no reason to get up in the mornings, no reason to put on a shirt and tie and make sure your appearance was neat and tidy, neither did they mention how old and useless you suddenly felt.

Her father had always been a busy and active man, until his retirement from the library, and for the last year Sarah had watched him as he became aware of all the things he no longer had without his job to go to. But Jason's arrival had changed all that, he had seemed to have a purpose in life again. These two needed each other; she only wished Garrett could be made to see that too.

God, how she cursed what had happened between them last night! Without it she would have been able to meet Garrett on equal terms; now she felt that every time he looked at her he wouldn't see the capable schoolteacher fighting for the happiness of two people she loved very much, but the wanton he had held in his arms the previous night.

'Damn, damn, damn!' She slammed the cupboard door shut after putting away the breakfast things.

'Something upsetting you on this bright and beautiful morning?'

She spun around to glare at the man causing her all this anguish, her eyes narrowing as he leant casually against the door-frame. She had been so engrossed in watching Jason and her father that she hadn't heard the arrival of Garrett's car or his entrance to the cottage, and now she had been put in exactly the position she hadn't wanted—on the defensive.

If her night had been spent restlessly then Garrett's obviously hadn't. There was none of the tiredness in his relaxed demeanour that had been so obvious the night before, and the lines about his eyes and mouth had softened too. Dressed as he was, in denims and a short-sleeved shirt, he looked for all the world as if he had just come to spend a lazy day with them!

'Have you had breakfast?' Sarah asked moodily.

'Eggs, bacon, sausages——'

'I didn't ask for the details.' She gave an inward shudder, her stomach protesting just at the thought of the greasy food.

'You obviously haven't eaten,' Garrett drawled, eyeing her mockingly. 'Don't you know that breakfast is the most important meal of the day?'

She swallowed, her stomach definitely delicate this morning. 'I'll make mine lunch today.'

He looked her over consideringly. 'No wonder

there's hardly anything of you if you don't eat.'

Sarah resisted the impulse to put her hands shieldingly over her body, the denim cut-offs seeming to expose a little too much of her legs today, even if the loose shirt was an improvement on the bikini top of yesterday. Knowing Garrett was coming here, she would have dressed a little more formally if she hadn't thought it might cause her father to speculate on the change from her usual attire.

'I've always been tiny,' she defended.

'Don't worry,' taunted Garrett. 'You aren't tiny where it matters.'

She had always thought the fullness of her breasts out of line with her other slenderness, and now that this man had seen her, touched her, she thought so even more. 'Garrett, about last night——'

'I wonder how many conversations, over the years, have started with those three words?' he drawled.

He was playing a damned cat-and-mouse game with her, and like a fool she had walked right into it, too embarrassed by her actions to avoid it, wanting what had happened between them out of the way. 'I don't care about other conversations, only this one,' she snapped. 'And last night you——'

'Kissed you,' he finished softly. 'And you kissed me right back,' he added huskily.

She gasped. 'I didn't encourage you!'

'You didn't try and stop me either,' he shrugged.

'That is hardly the point,' she protested. 'One second we were talking and the next you were proving how macho you are!'

His mouth twisted at the description. 'There are plenty of other women I could have done that with, ones who would involve fewer complications.'

Her eyes flashed. 'Then why did you kiss me?'

'Maybe because I wanted to see if the little she-cat was really as grown-up as she appeared,' he derided.

She stiffened as he used that description of her a second time. 'And?'

He moved further into the room. 'You know, I received some very strange looks when I arrived at the airport that day.' His eyes were narrowed as he watched her father and Jason out of the window, before suddenly turning to her. 'You left your scratch marks all the way down my cheek,' he remembered.

He was so close she could feel the heat of his body, and she hated the intimacy he had forced between them that had made her aware of that. 'You were breaking my father's heart!'

His mouth thinned. 'I was taking Jason home where he belonged.'

'And my father had just buried his elder daughter,' her eyes were over-bright at the memory, 'your *wife*!'

Garrett drew in a harsh breath at the accusation

in her tone. 'I was sorry that Amanda died the way she did——'

'Why were you?' Sarah challenged. 'It saved you having to go through the divorce!'

His eyes were flinty. 'There would have been no divorce.'

'Amanda had left you,' she scorned disbelievingly. 'The next step would obviously have been a divorce.'

'Not necessarily,' he grated. 'Certainly not between Amanda and me.'

Sarah frowned at his certainty. 'But Amanda had left you——'

'She would have come back,' he assured her arrogantly. 'She always did.'

'Always?' Sarah gave him a startled look. 'But——'

'How are they getting on together?' He nodded in the direction of her father and Jason, his expression grim.

She followed his gaze, a troubled frown still marring her brow. Amanda had never left Garrett before that last fateful time, so why had Garrett claimed she had? If he was trying to make her think badly of her sister he was out of luck; she had loved and admired Amanda, and she always would. She certainly wasn't going to take this man's word against her beloved sister.

'Fine,' she nodded abruptly. 'You very often find that the old and young do get on together.'

His mouth twisted. 'It's only us poor devils in between that have a rocky time of it!'

She looked at him coldly. 'I've never been aware of you trying to be likeable!'

His smile was spontaneous, his eyes warm, crinkled at the corners. 'Liking is such a lukewarm emotion.'

'Don't worry,' she scorned. 'There aren't too many people who feel such an undefined emotion about you!'

His expression softened as he gazed down at the beauty of her heart-shaped face. 'You grew up into a very beautiful woman, Sarah,' he told her softly. 'Your husband was a fool to ever let you go.'

He had answered her earlier question, and now she wished he hadn't; the last thing she wanted was to *feel* beautiful in his company. Beauty was, after all, only an illusion, as his attraction was; it was what a person was inside that mattered.

'Did you come to a decision concerning Jason?' She determinedly changed the subject.

'Not yet.' He looked at her consideringly. 'You shouldn't believe everything he tells you Sarah,' he added drily. 'Fifteen-year-old boys are apt to think the whole world is against them.'

She knew that, and she had already told Jason that she didn't like even the minor deceptions he had given them yesterday about his situation in London. Like all teenagers, he hadn't been too thrilled at the rebuke, but he had to know that at least one of them wasn't going to believe every hard-luck story he chose to tell them. And it was better that she be the one to show him that, since his friendship with his grandfather was already firmly cemented.

'I told you, I'm a teacher, I understand that,' she said stiffly. 'Nevertheless, I think he and my father would be good for each other if you allowed him to stay here for a while.'

'We'll see,' Garrett nodded non-committally. 'What's your subject?'

'Sorry?' she blinked.

'What do you teach?'

'Art,' she supplied abruptly.

He nodded, as if her answer came as no surprise to him. 'You painted the portraits of Amanda and your mother that are in the lounge.'

He hadn't commented on the portraits in the sitting-room the previous night, and so she had thought he hadn't seen them. She should have known this man didn't miss anything! 'They were gifts for my father,' she supplied reluctantly.

'They're very good,' Garrett told her in a bored voice. 'A little over-emotional, but then you're an emotional woman.'

'Garrett——'

'Did I say something wrong?' He raised innocent brows, his eyes mocking.

He knew that he had, had deliberately baited her. She wasn't normally an emotionally charged woman, in fact, she had often been called the opposite. Only this man evoked this response from her. 'Shall we join my father and Jason?' she suggested stiffly.

'Why bother?' Garrett shrugged. 'They seem to

be managing just fine without us.'

Her father and Jason didn't seem to have stopped talking the whole of the time they had been outside; but she wasn't 'managing' at all well without them as a buffer between her and Garrett! 'I'm sure Jason will want to see you,' she insisted firmly.

Garrett chuckled, a throaty sound that disturbed Sarah's already frayed nerves. 'I'm equally sure I'm the last person he wants to see,' he derided softly. 'Jason possesses all the acting talent of his mother, and there's nothing he likes more than a captive audience!'

'Aren't you being a little unfair to him?' Sarah defended. 'I'm sure his aunt and uncle are very nice, but he doesn't seem to like the way that he's always left with them.'

'He only stays with them during vacation time, and I really don't go away that much,' corrected Garrett grimly. 'His main objection to staying with them is that he's bored out of his mind. Jonathan is obviously very busy,' he added harshly. 'And Shelley isn't used to being around children of any age, let alone a bored teenager. She does the best she can in the circumstances, but it isn't good enough for Jason!'

'You're his father, you should——'

'I do the best I can too,' he flared. 'Like any other single parent who goes out to work.'

'Garrett, I don't want to argue with you——'

'It will be the first time,' he said. 'Even as a ten-year-old you argued with me about your choice of ice-cream!'

Sarah's cheeks flamed as she recalled that day during his first visit here, when he had taken them all for a drive into the country. She had been feeling very disturbed by the intrusion of this man into their lives, and the effect he was having on her parents, and he either hadn't heard her request for a chocolate ice-cream or he hadn't been paying attention. The result was a vanilla ice-cream that she had flatly refused to eat. She had been sent to her room as soon as they got home, but she had remained unrepentant.

Sixteen years later she could feel embarrassed about her behaviour. 'I was angry with you for marrying my sister,' she mumbled. 'You were an intruder, and I didn't like you.'

'You still don't,' he drawled. 'But I suggest we call a truce in front of Jason,' he advised softly as her father and his son turned back towards the house.

If she had expected him to spend a little time with Jason, make his decision, and then leave, either with Jason or without him, she was mistaken!

Father and son greeted each other stiffly, Jason defiantly announcing that his grandfather had offered to take him fishing. A censorious glance at her father had received an awkward shrug in return, and Sarah realised that once again her father's exuberance at being with his grandson had got the better of him.

'Why don't we all go?' Garrett suggested smoothly. 'I'm sure Sarah could pack us some food?'

The last thing she wanted was to be out on their twenty-six-foot cruiser with Garrett Kingham. But to have refused would have been to have ruined everyone else's fun, and so she nodded reluctant agreement to the idea.

There could be no doubt that *Garrett* was having fun, and most of it at her expense!

He helped her get the food ready while her father and Jason went in search of the fishing rods and other equipment. He stood far too close for comfort, meeting her gaze often in the driving mirror as they drove down to the boat in his hired Mercedes, letting his hand linger against her bikini-topped back as he helped her aboard the boat, sitting beside her on the padded seat at the back of the boat as her father and Jason took the controls.

To an outsider they must have looked like a family on an outing together, and Sarah's mouth tightened as she turned to find Garrett watching her with amused eyes. He seemed perfectly relaxed, his long legs stretched out in front of him, his hair golden in the bright sunshine. Sarah, very conscious of his gaze moving slowly over her body, was glad of her sunglasses to hide the thoughts revealed in her own eyes.

'You have a lovely sun-tan,' he drawled finally.

She shivered even in the heat of the day. 'Don't

you think there are enough problems between us without this?'

'Problems?' He looked about them pointedly, at the sun shining, the gulls crying overhead, the boat moving smoothly through the water, and best of all her father and Jason laughing together at the wheel of the boat.

'You know what I mean, Garrett,' she sighed. 'My father is being polite to you because he wants to be with Jason, but he has far from forgiven you for the misery you brought into all our lives.'

'All of them?' Garrett repeated softly, his eyes narrowed. 'What did I ever do to you?'

How could she explain that after Amanda died she had tried to be both herself and Amanda for her father, to help ease his pain, that she had hoped her own marriage would give him the grandchildren he lacked, and that even that had gone wrong? It seemed they had all been on a downward spiral ever since Garrett had first entered their lives.

'You destroyed my family,' she told him rigidly. 'You dazzled Amanda with your wealth and success, and succeeded in ruining three other lives at the same time.'

His gaze was icy. 'I'm relieved to hear that you don't include my son in that count,' he rasped softly.

'I'm reserving judgment,' she snapped. 'I just want you to realise that I don't need your unwelcome advances to tell me how obnoxious you are!' She glared at him, her eyes over-bright.

He stood up forcefully, moving forward to join the other two.

Sarah breathed easily for the first time since he had arrived at the cottage this morning. He knew that when he flirted with her it greatly disturbed her, had been doing it just to annoy her. And like a gauche child she had been annoyed. God, some of her pupils could have given him a better set-down than she had! It was only because it was Garrett Kingham doing the flirting that she felt this lack of control, she knew that; she just couldn't remain unaffected by the man who had been her sister's husband.

Why was he doing this to her? What satisfaction did it give him to hurt their family even more? Hadn't he done enough when he had made Amanda so unhappy she had finally been forced to leave him, to run from him, bringing their son with her! He was wrong when he said there would have been no divorce; Amanda had been talking about that very thing the day she died, her beautiful eyes flashing angrily.

They dropped anchor in a cove further up the coast, her father and Jason returning to their fishing immediately all the food had been consumed. Garrett remained at the back of the boat, Sarah very conscious of him as she cleared away.

'Please feel free to join them,' she finally invited jerkily, indicating the other two lying on the front of the boat half asleep, half fishing.

'What was he like?' Garrett suddenly asked interestedly, his arms folded across his chest.

She gave a start of surprise. 'What was who like?' she frowned.

'Your husband. David, I think you said his name was.' He watched her curiously.

Her hands shook slightly as she continued to pack away. 'He's a teacher, like me.'

Light brows rose. 'You work together at the same school?' he probed.

She shook her head. 'We were both still training when we met. David lives and works in London now.'

Garrett's eyes narrowed. 'How long were the two of you married?'

'Not long,' she avoided. 'Why the sudden interest in my marriage, Garrett?' she queried lightly.

'It isn't sudden,' he shrugged. 'I've been interested ever since you told me about it.'

'Why?'

'I'm curious about the ten years of your life since we last met, and your marriage seems to be as good a place to start as any,' he drawled.

'Well, I can assure you that my marriage was only a small part of that,' she dismissed, thrusting her hands into the pockets at the back of her denim cut-offs now that the picnic-basket had been repacked.

'How small a part?'

'Really, Garrett——'

'I'm not asking for the fun of it, Sarah.' He grasped her arms, pulling her down on to the seat beside him. 'Women who have—been married—

don't usually shy away from physical contact with a man the way that you do,' he explained grimly.

Her eyes flashed. 'Meaning I'm supposed to be hungry for any man who shows me the slightest interest, even you?'

'I didn't say that——'

'You implied it,' she said, glaring at him with furious blue eyes.

'Sarah——'

'Why don't you just leave me alone?' Tears glistened in her eyes. 'I don't want you to even touch me, I don't want——'

'*Sarah*!' he groaned, throatily, his mouth fast descending towards hers.

This was wrong, so very wrong. She hated this man, despised him. But she was returning his kiss as if her very life depended on it!

His hair felt silky soft as her fingers became entangled in it, his cheeks hard, his jaw firm. He was beautiful, and she wanted him, so very much. A sob caught in her throat as his mouth left hers.

His eyes were dark and stormy. 'Let's go down below,' he urged huskily.

'My father and Jason——'

'Are both asleep,' he assured her gruffly. 'Please, Sarah!'

'But——'

'Sarah, I have to touch you!' he groaned, opening the cabin door and pushing her inside.

It was a small cabin, just room for a small kitchen area and the two bunk beds on either side at the front. It was to one of these that Garrett led her, sitting down beside her on its narrow length.

'I've been thinking about touching you again ever since your father walked in on us last night,' he told her savagely. 'If he hadn't interrupted——'

'But he did,' Sarah said weakly. 'And maybe we should be grateful that he did.'

'No,' Garrett denied grimly. 'I want you, Sarah, and I think you want me too.'

'No——'

'*Yes*,' he insisted as his head lowered to hers once more.

Tears scalded her cheeks even as she returned the heat of his kiss, and she hated herself for responding to him and yet was unable to stop herself.

This was the reason she hated Garrett, the reason her marriage to David had never stood a chance, because it was *Garrett* she loved, whom she had always loved!

CHAPTER FOUR

SARAH had only been a child when she first met Garrett, but in her own way she had had a crush on him even then, that crush only turning to hate when she saw how unhappy he made Amanda. And it had been the hate that dominated every time she saw him after that, her love for him firmly buried beneath that resentment, so firmly buried that even she had believed it to be dead.

Until last night.

Last night, as he had kissed her and touched her, he had shown her that she wasn't cold and frigid with a man, as she had always believed she was, that she just needed the *right* man to touch her. Garrett was that man.

Through the long hours of the night as she lay awake she had tried to deny that knowledge even to herself, had convinced herself that she still hated him, that she would always hate him, that she couldn't possibly love a man like him.

But she did, knew it even as she arched her throat so that his lips might trail moistly down to the valley between her breasts, catching her breath in her throat as his lips closed moistly over one pebble-hard nipple through her bikini top, trembling as she felt the gentle drawing motion of his mouth.

God, the aching torture of his caress, the hunger she felt for even more than he was giving!

And then she felt a cool draught of air against her heated flesh as her bikini top was deftly undone and as quickly thrown aside. She gazed up at Garrett longingly as he lowered her back on the bed, not caring at that moment that Jason and her father lay above them on the foredeck of the boat, that either of them could decide to come and investigate their disappearance at any moment.

'You're beautiful, Sarah,' Garrett told her huskily, his eyes dark. 'So beautiful and—oh God, I want you!' he choked, his thighs lying across hers as he moved down to claim her mouth in a fiery kiss.

Her back arched in a primitive need for possession as his hand cupped her naked breast and the heated tip knew his sure caress; her arms entwined about his neck as the kiss deepened and deepened.

She was lost, completely beyond control, whimpering for his full possession.

'Not here, Sarah,' he murmured regretfully, the fiery passion in his own eyes telling her of his need. 'But soon, my love, soon,' he promised raggedly. 'But I have to help you dress now, or else——'

Oh God, oh God, what was she doing? What had she almost done!

She swung up and away from him, clasping her bikini top to her, her cheeks chalky-white.

'Sarah——'

'Don't—touch—me,' she told him in a carefully controlled voice.

'Don't hate yourself, darling,' he soothed. 'It was beautiful. We——'

'It's *you* I hate.' She glared at him. 'You with your money and your power, and your damned certainty that you can have whatever and *whoever* you want!' She fastened her top with the sureness of habit, standing up shakily. 'Let me pass,' she ordered as Garrett deliberately stood in front of her.

His expression was pleading. 'Sarah——'

'I said, let me pass, Garrett,' she bit out viciously, marching outside into the fresh air as he did so, only just reaching the side before she completely lost the lunch she had consumed such a short time ago.

She loved a man who had seduced her sister and got her pregnant, had hurt her parents, destroyed his marriage, alienated Jason from them for years, and who used the words 'my love' and 'darling' in an effort to seduce *her*!

There was no rhyme or reason for her love for Garrett, it just was, it always had been, and she hated herself for it even if she could no longer hate *him*.

God, how amusing he must find it to realise, as he believed, that she was just another frustrated divorcee who burned in his arms after all!

Her stomach was still heaving even though there was nothing left in it, but she welcomed that ache so that she could block out the pain of self-disgust in her chest.

'Hey, what happened to you?' Jason called with some concern.

She wiped her face with a handerkerchief, attempting to smile as she turned towards him. 'It's typical of me,' she derided. 'I get sea-sick as soon as we drop anchor!' She avoided her father's puzzled gaze, both of them knowing she had never been sea-sick in her life. But it had been the best she could come up with at such short notice. How could she explain that she was *self*-sick, and that the grim-faced man standing in the cabin doorway was the cause!

'Maybe we should go back,' her father suggested uncertainly.

'I don't want to spoil anything——'

'Maybe we *should* go back now, Geoffrey,' Garrett put in harshly. 'I have to drive back to London today.'

His reminder that he was taking Jason away with him when he went made them all quiet on the drive back to the cottage. Sarah carefully avoided all further contact with him.

After today she would probably never have to see Garrett again, and yet the thought that that would probably include Jason for some time too depressed her greatly. Garrett was a heartless, egotistical swine, and she hated what he made her feel. She only wished she could still hate *him*.

He made no effort to get out of the car once they reached the cottage, the engine still running too. 'I won't bother to come in,' he rasped. 'It's a long

drive back. Stay, Jason,' he instructed as he would
have got out of the car.

Jason looked rebellious, the uneasy truce that
had existed between father and son all day already
over as far as he was concerned. 'I have to go in and
get my things——'

'No need,' his father bit out. 'You'll be staying
on with your grandfather and Sarah for a few
days.'

'I will?' Jason looked as disbelieving as Sarah
and her father felt.

Garrett nodded abruptly. 'I'll come back for
you at the weekend. But I wanted to have a talk to
you first,' he added grimly.

'Thank you, Garrett.' Sarah's father squeezed
his shoulder. 'It means a lot to me.'

'Sarah convinced me of that.' Green eyes looked
at her coldly. 'I won't keep Jason long,' he assured
the other man.

Sarah felt as if Garrett had just struck her. Did
he really believe she had allowed him to touch her
the way that he had because she hoped to persuade
him to leave Jason here? Didn't he realise she
would have stopped him if she could!

'I never thought he would agree,' her father
grinned as he put the kettle on. 'I don't know what
you said to him, Sarah, but I thank you for it.'

He might not feel quite so grateful if he realised
what price Garrett believed she had almost paid
for it! 'I didn't say anything to him, Dad. You
know Garrett.' Her mouth tightened. 'No one can
make up his mind for him.'

'No.' He frowned thoughtfully. 'What happened to you out there today?' he asked concernedly. 'I've never known you to be seasick before.'

'Maybe it was something I ate, because I feel fine now,' she lied, her stomach still churning at the wanton way she had responded to Garrett.

'Strange, the rest of us have suffered no ill effects, and we all ate the same things. Although, now that I think about it,' he frowned, 'Garrett looked a little pale after lunch too.'

'How could you tell under all that tan?' she derided harshly. Garrett's bronzed skin was a startling contrast to the lightness of his hair.

'Now then, Sarah,' her father chided. 'You're pretty tanned yourself at the moment.'

But Garrett's skin was always that tanned, and when she was younger she had spent hours fantasising what it must be like to touch that skin, envying her sister her husband. Until he had broken the heart of everyone she held most dear. Then her fantasies had taken a completely different turn, all of them becoming vengeful.

But the love had survived. She didn't know how or why, it just wouldn't die.

'What do you suppose he wanted to say to Jason?' Her father frowned worriedly.

She grimaced. 'Probably much the same as I said to him this morning: that he acted irresponsibly, without any thought for others, and that if he does it again he won't go unpunished.'

Her father chuckled. 'So that's why he couldn't

eat his breakfast!'

Sarah eyed him reprovingly. 'I should have said the same to you,' she warned him. 'Although I realise that Jason did mislead you a little about the circumstances.'

'Thank you,' he teased.

'It could have had serious consequences, Dad——'

'But it didn't.' He squeezed her arm reassuringly as the front door closed behind Jason. 'Now let's try and make it a pleasant stay for the boy, hm?'

'All right,' she agreed slowly. 'But I won't let you spoil him.'

Blue eyes gleamed with laughter. 'I didn't think for one moment that you would!'

Sarah gave Jason a bright smile as he came into the sitting-room, as anxious as her father that he shouldn't sense that anything was wrong. But as she prepared tea for them all, she and her father ignoring the fact that Jason had been a little red-faced when he came in, she couldn't get her thoughts off the fact that in three days' time Garrett would be back.

Three days wasn't a lot of time to make up for ten years' separation, but the three of them did their best, swimming together, going out fishing on the boat again, going into town to do some shopping a couple of times too. Their evenings were spent quietly, her father and Jason discovering they both had a passion for chess. It was during those quiet evenings at home that Garrett called his son,

Sarah always making sure Jason or her father answered those calls, having no wish to even speak to him.

Although there had been one or two things which had disturbed her, and which she wished she *could* talk to him about. A couple of times she had noticed the same man when they went out or were on the beach, and after what Garrett had told her about kidnapping——! But it was ridiculous to suppose that innocuous-looking man was involved in anything like that—wasn't it? She told herself Garrett was making her as nervous as he obviously was, that the poor man was probably just on holiday and probably hadn't even noticed the amount of times they had all been in the same place at the same time.

In those three short days, Jason became deeply interwoven into their lives, his reserve gone as he forgot how grown-up he was trying to appear. The time passed all too quickly, and on the last evening, Jason lingered over going to bed, although his grandfather had succumbed to tiredness half an hour ago and retired to his room.

'I hope I didn't upset you the day I arrived.' Jason looked at Sarah uncertainly.

She put down her sewing. 'All I can remember about that day is being pleased to see you,' she assured him.

He shrugged his shoulders uncomfortably. 'I was dumb to think you could be my mother.'

Sarah frowned. 'Why did you? Surely your father told you she was dead?'

'Sure,' he nodded. 'But you looked so much like her and—all I can remember about my mother is that she just disappeared one day, and then there was just Dad and me.' He sighed. 'I thought—for a moment that day, I thought maybe he had only told me she was dead because the two of them had separated and he didn't want me to see her.' He looked a little sheepish.

That wasn't really so far from the truth, but it had been Amanda's family Garrett had kept him away from. But it was good that he didn't remember the tragedy of his mother's death, or the scene that had followed in this very cottage.

But it bothered her that he kept saying she looked like Amanda. She didn't—did she?

'In a way I'm sorry that isn't what happened, rather than your mother dying,' she said gently. 'Although I can assure you that Amanda would never have stayed out of your life for ten years; she loved you too much ever to agree to that.'

Jason looked wistful. 'All I can remember about her is a beautiful lady who used to bring me presents.'

'You were her whole world,' Sarah told him softly.

He stood up. 'I'm glad I came here, that I spent time with you and Grandad. I—I'm going to miss you both,' he burst out before almost running from the room and up the stairs to his bedroom.

They were going to miss him too, and she knew her father was dreading the parting tomorrow. But he was also grateful to Garrett for giving them those few days; Sarah's own feelings towards Garrett were still deeply resentful.

And she was also bothered by what Jason had just said, and stood up to look at herself in the mirror.

The mirror reflected a deeply tanned young woman with flyaway black hair and troubled blue eyes.

Her breath caught in her throat as the portrait of Amanda on the opposite wall was reflected beside her, her sister as she had looked shortly before her death. The similarities were startling, if only superficial.

Had Garret seen those similarities too—had that been the reason he seemed compelled to touch her, the reason he had kissed her? He and Amanda hadn't seemed especially happy together, in fact the opposite, but Garrett had claimed that had Amanda lived there would have been no divorce between them. Not all couples who loved each other could live happily together, in fact some people found it impossible to do so; and perhaps in his own way Garrett had loved Amanda. Perhaps he had also seen her as a suitable substitute!

His kiss that first night had come after an argument about Amanda having left him, and the next day his mood had seemed almost buoyant, as if something greatly pleased him.

It would be a complete turnabout from thinking he and Amanda had been unhappy together, and yet as she looked in the mirror again the evidence was right in front of her eyes; for a brief time she had become Amanda for him.

Not knowing when he was going to arrive the next day, the three of them spent the day on the beach near the cottage, but by late afternoon Garrett still hadn't arrived.

But the man Sarah had noticed on several of their other outings had settled himself in a cove up the beach from them. The coincidence seemed too much of one this time, as she found him watching them every time she happened to glance at him. Her father and Jason seemed unaware of their observer, but as the afternoon wore on and the beach began to empty the man remained exactly where he was. And Sarah's unease deepened.

Without giving herself time to think, Sarah left her father and Jason to their swim, marching the short distance across the beach it took to stand in front of the man. He looked up at her curiously, and Sarah wondered if she could be making a mistake; he certainly didn't look like a kidnapper, not much taller than herself, with a whipcord thinness that could at best be described as wiry, his sparse brown hair neatly combed, his brown eyes coolly assessing.

It was his eyes that made her stance remain one of challenge. 'I don't know what you hope to gain by spying on us in this way,' she snapped. 'But I want you to realise I know exactly what you're doing.'

Light brows rose. 'Really?'

His voice struck a chord in her memory, but

before she could decide where she had heard it before, the sand beneath her left foot began to move, collapsing into the hole the man had been digging beside him. Her balance gone, Sarah's expression was one of horror as she felt herself falling towards him.

His reactions were quick, his hands coming up to catch her, but even so his breath left his body in a whoosh as she landed in an undignified heap of arms and legs on top of him.

'Really, Dennis,' drawled an amused voice that was so infuriatingly familiar. 'I know I asked you to keep an eye on them, but I meant from a distance!'

Sarah recovered enough to turn and look at Garrett, her cheeks colouring at the mockery on his face, before she turned back to the man who still lay beneath her. 'Dennis?' she repeated disbelievingly.

'Right,' he snapped in that gravelly voice that was so deceptive of his size and appearance. 'If you wouldn't mind getting off me, Mrs Croft?' he added disgustedly.

She scrambled inelegantly to her feet, brushing the sand from her bikini-clad body, keeping her gaze averted from both men, too mortified to look at either of them.

Dennis stood up too, four inches taller than her at the most, his mouth twisting wryly as she couldn't help but gape at him. 'When you grow up in a neighbourhood like mine, with a name like Dennis, you grow up tough or you don't grow up at all.' The last was added in a hard tone.

She swallowed hard. 'I'm sorry. I—I had no idea Garrett had sent you here.' Or she would never have made such a fool of herself, her glare in Garrett's direction clearly told him.

'Jason is my responsibility,' Dennis rasped, before turning to Garrett. 'She came right over and challenged me, boss.' He frowned heavily. 'She thought I was after Jason.'

Garrett drew in a harsh breath, grasping Sarah's arm to pull her over to stand beside him. 'Thanks, Dennis,' he bit out, pulling Sarah along at his side, his expression grim.

She had been dreading this meeting, but she certainly hadn't expected it to turn out like this. Garrett looked furious, as if he would like to put her over his knee and spank her. As he put up an acknowledging hand to Jason and her father as they still cavorted in the water, completely unaware of the scene that had just transpired on the beach, all the time continuing to walk towards the cottage, Sarah had a terrible feeling that was exactly what he did intend to do!

'Garrett!' she snapped, trying to pull free but only succeeding in bruising her arm. 'Garrett, let me go!' she ordered.

'No,' came his uncompromising reply.

They were barely through the front door before Garrett turned her to face him, his fingers biting into the tops of her arms as he glowered down at her. 'You little fool,' he rasped. 'You damned little fool!'

Before Sarah could voice her indignation her lips were claimed in a savage kiss meant to punish, her body crushed against his, the sand and sea-water soiling the beige trousers and shirt he wore.

The kiss went on and on, punishing, dominating, laying claim, and although Sarah felt weak from the force of it all she knew it couldn't continue.

She wrenched her mouth away from his, pushing ineffectually at his chest. 'I'm not Amanda!' she finally burst out, able to move away from him as he became suddenly still.

His eyes were dark as he looked at her searchingly. 'Is that the reason you've created for yourself for my kissing you?' he finally rasped. 'That I pretend you're *Amanda*?'

'Well, isn't it?' she challenged, her eyes flashing.

'No,' he answered flatly.

'But——'

'I know exactly who you are every second I kiss and touch you,' he bit out harshly. 'Can you say the same thing?'

She frowned her puzzlement. 'What——'

'Do you pretend I'm your ex-husband?' Garrett grated, his body tense.

'No, of course not,' she denied instantly; she had *never* responded to David the way she did to Garrett. 'And I've never kissed you to persuade you to leave Jason here either,' she told him heatedly.

'I was angry with you when I said that,' he dismissed. 'I'm not used to women actually being sick after I've made love to them!' he added grimly.

'That was because——'

'Of who I am, not what we did,' he cut in raspingly. 'But we respond to *each other*, Sarah, not because of Amanda, or David. And I don't intend fighting the emotions you arouse in me, it makes me feel too damned good for me to do that,' he added huskily. 'It's a long time since I felt that!'

She swallowed hard. 'Surely the way I make you feel is irrelevant?' she said breathlessly. 'You and Jason will be leaving today.'

'Tomorrow,' he corrected abruptly. 'I've booked into a hotel overnight,' he explained softly.

'Well, then——'

'I've given up too much of what I wanted to let you go too,' he cut in determinedly. 'We'll be together, Sarah, you can depend on it!'

She didn't want to depend on it, wanted him far away from her, when hopefully she would be able to forget her love for him once again. 'I don't think so,' she denied coldly.

He put a hand up to his eyes, rubbing them as if they ached. 'I haven't been able to think straight since I came here the other night and saw you again,' he rasped. 'I wish I could make you see, understand——'

'I *saw*,' she cut in scornfully. 'And I *understood* that you made my sister miserable!'

His eyes flashed dangerously. 'I was just as unhappy.'

'That's often what happens when you're forced to face up to the responsibility of making an eighteen-year-old girl pregnant!' She glared at him.

He flinched as if she had physically struck him. 'I think I'll go and join Jason and Geoffrey,' he said at last with deadly calm.

Sarah was still breathing hard once he had gone outside, small sobs catching in her throat. Why couldn't she have wanted David the way she undoubtedly wanted Garrett; why did she have to want the one man she couldn't have?

Dinner was a strained affair, her father and Jason obviously feeling the parting deeply, so lost in their own misery that they seemed unaware of the tension between Sarah and Garrett.

But Sarah was aware of it, knew that although Garrett appeared as coolly controlled as he usually was he used every excuse he could manufacture to touch her, that if she trembled at the touch his hands shook in return. He really, genuinely wanted her, couldn't help himself. And she couldn't have him.

'Care for a walk outside, Sarah?' he suggested after they had cleared away and her father and Jason were once again locked in battle over the chessboard.

She instantly felt hunted. 'Er—no, I don't think so. I have some sewing to do, and ——'

'You're looking pale, Sarah,' her father cut in, showing that not all of his attention had been given to his next move after all. 'Some fresh air might make you feel better.'

'I've been out in the fresh air all day,' she dismissed lightly, evading Garrett's compelling gaze.

'Then just keep me company,' he persuaded huskily.

He had put her in such a position that she would look rude if she refused! Damn him. 'I'll just get a cardigan,' she accepted abruptly, hurrying from the room.

They walked in silence for several minutes, Sarah very aware of him, shivering with expectation when his arm occasionaly brushed against her. She felt as if she were on fire, her thoughts racing, a wild fluttering in the region of her heart.

'Geoffrey and Jason have got on well together, then?' Garrett finally spoke as they stood at the water's edge.

She smiled. 'Extremely well.' She sighed. 'Dad will miss him once he's gone.'

'Hm,' Garrett frowned. 'I'm afraid my own father's idea of being a grandparent is an expensive present at Christmas and birthdays, and a lecture on upholding the Kingham name every time they meet!'

She grimaced. 'I'm afraid we haven't been much better over the years.'

Garrett looked at her in the fading light. 'Jason

realises that wasn't through any choice of yours or your father's.'

'I'm sure your father is a very busy man——'

'Oh, yes,' he confirmed bitterly. 'He's always been that.'

'Garrett——'

'I can see a change in Jason in just three days,' he said softly. 'He was becoming a petulant brat. I've certainly never seen him do the dishes the way he did with us tonight!'

'That's probably because you have a house-keeper, and he——'

'It isn't just that,' Garrett shook his head, 'Jason's whole attitude is less selfish.'

'I'm glad if you think being here has helped him in some way.' She turned away. 'Where's Dennis tonight?'

'At the hotel,' he said tersely. 'You really were very stupid this afternoon,' he added grimly. 'What if Dennis really had been after Jason? He could have had a gun——'

'A gun?' she echoed in a sickened voice.

'I'm sorry.' Garrett frowned heavily at how pale her face had become. 'I've lived all my life in a society where guns are easily accessible, I forgot how different things are over here.'

'It isn't so different in England any more.' She shook her head. 'We get our own share of pointless killings, violence for violence's sake. I just——it was the thought of something happening to Jason.'

'It's all right, Sarah,' his arms closed about her

firmly, 'I'm not going to let anything happen to either of you. Ever.'

She couldn't allow him to keep saying these things to her, too much stood between them. 'Please let me go, Garrett,' she ordered stiffly.

'Don't you think I would if I could?' he scorned self-derisively. 'The last thing I was looking for when I came here was involvement with any woman, let alone you!'

Because she was Amanda's sister. She had been right all along, this man had never loved Amanda! 'Then you don't have to worry, do you,' she dismissed roughly, glaring up at him. 'Because you aren't *going* to be involved with me!'

'I already am,' he told her softly.

'It takes two for an involvement, Garrett,' she bit out, trying to free herself as he refused to release her.

He looked down at her ruefully. 'And are you saying you aren't?'

'Of course I'm not.' She was breathing hard from the effort of trying to free herself. 'I don't like you, I've never liked you——'

'But you respond to me,' he insisted firmly. 'It's enough to start with.'

'No——'

'Yes!' he grated, his chest rapidly rising and falling. 'We both know we could lie down on the beach right this minute and you would let me take you!'

She quivered at the erotic image his words evoked; the two of them against the golden sand, their bodies entwined, joined—oh God. She trembled. She couldn't feel this way about Garrett, she *shouldn't*.

'We also know I'm not about to do that,' Garrett added raggedly, and Sarah was mortified at the disappointment she felt at the words. 'You're special, Sarah, and what's between us is special too, and when we make love there's going to be nothing clandestine about it.'

When they made love, not if, but when! Sarah pulled roughly out of his arms. 'All those little would-be actresses hoping for a part in one of your films may be anxious to share your bed, but I'm certainly not!' She glared at him with over-bright eyes.

'I've never even considered awarding parts in my films for "services rendered",' Garrett denied wearily.

'Not even to Amanda?' she challenged. 'Didn't she go to bed with you hoping you could help her career and end up pregnant with your child?'

His eyes narrowed to emerald slits. 'Is that what she told you happened?'

'I was only sixteen when she died, hardly old enough for her to have discussed the sex life between you with me,' Sarah scorned.

'If she *had* discussed it with you you would have realised that isn't the way it happened.'

'Amanda didn't love you——'

'No, but she wanted me,' he bit out harshly, his eyes cold as Sarah flinched.

'You didn't have to let her have you,' she cried

emotionally. 'She was eighteen. Garrett, Eighteen!'

He sighed, his hands thrust into his denims' pockets. 'I wish I could explain my marriage to Amanda——'

'I don't want to *know* about your marriage to my sister,' she disclaimed heatedly. 'It's enough that it ever existed!'

'Sarah——'

'Don't touch me again,' she warned tautly. 'Just say goodnight to my father and Jason and then go! I'll try to make sure I'm not around when you come for Jason tomorrow.' She turned on her heel and hurried back to the cottage.

She wanted to escape straight up to her bedroom, but she was aware of how odd it would look to her father and Jason if she disappeared so abruptly after walking on the beach with Garrett, so she stiffened her shoulders and went to join them in the sitting-room.

The game of chess was still in progress when she entered the room, and she took a few minutes to gaze indulgently at the two bent so intently over the board that they were unaware of her presence for the moment.

No matter how heart-wrenching it had been for her to see Garrett again, to be with him, it had been worth it to have Jason here with them. And when he and Garrett returned to America at least her father would have this memory to brighten up his days. Only her own memories of the visit wouldn't be as happy, and that had nothing to do with Jason's presence.

Her father glanced up after making the move that gave him checkmate. 'Did you leave Garrett outside?' he asked lightly.

'No, I'm here, Geoffrey.' Garrett stepped into the room behind her, brushing against her as he crossed the room to stand beside the unlit fireplace. 'Good game?' he asked pleasantly, acting for all the world as if he and Sarah hadn't just had another argument outside.

Her father nodded. 'I'm going to miss my chess partner,' he said regretfully.

'I have to get back to Los Angeles for a while,' Garrett explained softly. 'And I want Jason to come with me. I do have another idea, though,' he added huskily, speaking to her father but glancing often at Sarah as she stood rigidly across the room. 'Why don't the two of you come back with us for a holiday?'

Sarah felt as if all the breath had been knocked from her body, knowing by the excitement on her father and Jason's faces that they were thrilled at the idea, also knowing by the triumph in Garrett's expression that he had anticipated her own reluctance at such a suggestion and had deliberately put the idea in front of the others so that she wasn't able to voice it!

CHAPTER FIVE

A WEEK later, as she and her father left the plane at Los Angeles airport, Sarah was still wondering how she had let herself be persuaded into coming here. Not that it had actually been a case of persuasion, more of coercion!

After Garrett had dropped his bombshell that night she had come up with all kinds of objections as to why they couldn't possibly go to America at such short notice, all of them overridden by one male or another, usually her father. Garrett hadn't even had to do his arguing himself! It had been a losing battle, one she knew she had lost from the first, even if she did try to give a token fight.

Not that Garrett had had everything his own way. She had insisted that she and her father couldn't go straight away, that there were things to organise before they left the country. Garrett had readily agreed with her on that, mainly, she knew, because he had already won the major battle and could allow her the victory of the lesser one.

So here they were. And as soon as they had passed through Customs she was going to see Garrett again, having received a telephone call from him last night at their London hotel to tell them he would be meeting them himself. Sarah had let her father take the call, deliberately absenting herself from the room by taking a shower, although her father had excitedly informed her of the plans when she rejoined him in the lounge of their suite.

Her father was the sole reason she was taking this trip, and she hadn't liked to dampen his enthusiasm by coming out with any of the sarcastic comments that sprang so easily to mind.

Garrett had deliberately manoeuvred her into visiting his home because he was no longer able to try and seduce her in England. It seemed a little extreme to her, but she couldn't think of any other explanation for his actions; he had certainly never made the suggestion when Amanda was still alive. No, he had known exactly how her father would react to spending more time with his grandson, just as he had known she would have no choice but to accompany him.

'That was all very efficient, anyway,' her father remarked a short time later as they and their luggage went in search of Garrett.

Sarah was too tense to answer him, dreading seeing Garrett again, trembling with the effort it took for her to remain calm. Her father was too excited to notice what a nervous wreck she was!

She spotted Garrett in the crowd almost immediately, his hair gleaming golden in the sunshine as he towered over the people who surrounded him. Intense pleasure darkened his eyes as he took in her appearance, the elegant but cool linen dress that was the same colour blue as her eyes.

Almost before she was aware of it Garrett signalled the man at his side to take their luggage, giving her father's hand a firm shake before standing determinedly in front of her.

Apprehension darkened her eyes as she waited for his next move, and her breath left her body in a relieved sigh as he clasped her shoulders before bending to kiss her cheek in a totally brotherly way.

'Coward!' he accused softly before straightening, looking amused.

Her eyes flashed. If she really were a coward she would have found some way to avoid coming here, and let her father make this visit alone. But that would only have delayed seeing Garrett again; she had no doubt that if she hadn't come with her father today, he would have come to see her when he returned to London. Garrett wasn't a man who accepted no for an answer.

She had expected the humidity when they stepped out of the airport on to the pavement, but even so it was a little cloying. But they didn't have to wait in the sticky heat for long, the man who had taken their suitcases was standing beside a cream limousine, holding the back door open for them all to get in.

'I always wanted to travel in one of these,' Sarah's father said excitedly as he got in beside her, Garrett sitting on the other side of him on the long leather seat.

Sarah shot Garrett a look that told him clearly of her contempt for his obvious show of wealth. Her

father might be impressed but she certainly
wasn't, despite the luxury of the air-conditioned
car.

'The car belongs to the film studio,' Garrett
drawled. 'It was Jason's idea that we use it today,'
he added drily. 'I warned him that you would
probably find it as ostentatious as I do, but he
insisted.'

'I'm glad he did. Although you were right,'
chuckled her father. 'One of these would look
pretty silly parked outside the cottage!'

Sarah's brows rose mockingly. 'We could
always tell everyone it was a spare room!'

Garrett's mouth quirked. 'It's certainly big
enough to put a bed in the back!'

She turned away abruptly as a blush darkened
her cheeks, her mockery having neatly rebounded
on her. Nothing had changed in the last week.
Garrett still wanted her, the warmth in his eyes
before she turned away telling her that he wished
there *were* a bed in the back here with them!

'Where is Jason?' Her father frowned his
puzzlement. 'I expected him to be with you.'

'And he wanted to come,' Garrett nodded. 'But
I left him at the house playing host. I hope you
don't mind, but my father, brother and his wife
are staying with me at the moment too. They
might consider Los Angeles just a playground,' he
derided. 'But it's convenient for the ocean!'

Oh, this was great, Sarah stormed silently, not
just Garrett to contend with but the whole of the
Kingham family! She knew that Amanda had

found her father-in-law abrupt to the point of
rudeness, although she had seemed to get on well
enough with Jonathan and Shelley Kingham. As
far as Sarah was concerned this unwanted visit to
Garrett's home was becoming more and more of a
nightmare.

'Of course we don't mind, Garrett,' her father
dismissed lightly. 'We're the visitors here; you're
perfectly at liberty to invite your family to stay
with you.'

Garrett shrugged. 'It isn't a question of inviting
them; they often descend on me this time of year.'

Sarah couldn't help wishing that this year they
hadn't decided to do so. What could she and her
father possibly have in common with the powerful
Kinghams? They were, quite literally, involved
with this family by accident, wouldn't have been
given the time of day by them if Amanda hadn't
been Jason's mother. It wasn't that Sarah was a
snob, but Amanda had told her more than once
that the elder Kingham was, at least.

'I'm sure it will be fine,' her father assured
Garrett. 'Now tell me all the places of interest
along the way!' he encouraged eagerly.

Like her father, Sarah had never been outside
England before, and she listened without comment as Garrett pointed out places and things he
thought might interest them, including the
Chinese Theatre and the famous HOLLYWOOD
sign that everyone had seen at least once on their
television. But most of all she was interested in the
beauty of the place, the sunshine brighter than any

she had ever seen in England, the swaying palms, and the beautiful homes.

'What are those young people doing?' her father asked curiously.

Sarah had also noticed several teenagers at the side of the road selling something to the cars that were continually stopping before slowly driving on again, but she couldn't see what they were selling.

Garrett's lips turned back derisively. 'They're selling maps that are supposed to tell the general public exactly where the stars live!'

'How awful!' Sarah burst out disgustedly. 'And you mean people actually buy those maps so that they can go and intrude on someone's privacy?'

'I believe that is the general idea,' he drawled.

'I hope your home isn't one of the ones on the maps.' She shuddered at the thought of being gawked at like some peep-show.

He shook his head. 'As far as I know I'm not a "star",' he derided. 'Besides, this is Beverly Hills, and we live at Malibu. I only brought you here because I had strict instructions from Jason to make sure you saw all the sights on the way home.'

There was no doubt about the beauty of the homes in this area, although a lot of them were hidden behind high fences and hedgerows, iron gates, some of them even displaying a television camera so that visitors could be monitored before they reached the door. It seemed a pity to Sarah that the people who lived here couldn't be allowed to live in peace.

'I know what you're thinking, Sarah,' Garrett mused at her disgusted expression. 'But they don't have to live here.'

'I suppose not,' she acknowledged slowly. 'But it does seem a pity,' she insisted.

Garrett's house turned out to be right on the edge of the beach, a lovely *hacienda*-style house, painted a pristine white, long and rambling. It was a really beautiful house, and as they got out of the car Sarah could see a swimming-pool at the back, several palm trees edging the marble-sided water, and a man and woman in the cool depths.

It was just as beautiful inside as out, the décor luxurious and warm, the air cool and inviting, a rounded woman of obvious Latin heritage greeting them inside the door, informing them that Jason and Senator Kingham Senior were down in the games-room, and that Senator Kingham Junior and Mrs Kingham were out in the pool, which confirmed the identity of the couple Sarah had seen outside.

'I'll take you to your rooms,' Garrett smiled. 'Then we can all have a drink by the pool and I'll introduce you to everyone.'

Sarah's father's bedroom was the height of luxury, in beige and browns, and yet hers turned out to be even more so, the pale green and cream décor very beautiful. Her luggage had already been placed in the room, and she longed to change out of the linen dress into something a little more comfortable in the heat of the day. But Garrett still stood inside the room. She looked at him enquiringly, her head back in challenge.

He held her gaze steadily as he quietly closed the door behind him, crossing the room to stand mere inches in front of her.

When he stood this close she felt utterly helpless, even the three-inch heels on her sandals did not give her enough height to be able to look at him with any degree of confidence.

His hands came up to cradle each side of her flushed face. 'I never realised I could miss anyone as much as I've missed you this last week!'

Sarah's breath left her in a heady gasp. If he had been aggressive or demanding she would have had no difficulty in resisting him, but he barely touched her, and his voice was a tortured groan. For ten years she hadn't even seen this man, but the past week apart had been unendurable for her too!

'Garrett——'

'Don't turn me away,' he pleaded raggedly, his gaze searching. He sighed his relief as he saw the vulnerability in her eyes. 'You missed me too!'

'I——'

'Lying about it won't change the truth I can see in your eyes,' he cajoled huskily.

She shook her head. 'What do you *want* from me?' she cried.

'Just you,' he groaned. 'I just want what you feel for me to show.'

'I thought it already did,' she snapped, stepping back from him. 'I despise you and what you put Amanda through when she lived with you.'

Garrett's expression darkened as his arms dropped back to his sides. He looked very attractive in the white trousers and dark green shirt. 'What did I put her through?' he rasped. 'Did I beat her? Did I have other women? What?' he demanded.

Sarah swallowed hard. She was sure Garrett had never struck a woman; his strength came from a far different source than brute force; and Amanda had never mentioned other women in his life. 'There are other forms of cruelty apart from the ones you just mentioned,' she insisted stubbornly.

Garrett's mouth tightened. 'You mean the fact that I went out to work so that we could continue to live in the luxury that Amanda loved so much?' he scorned.

'Amanda was never interested in your money,' she defended hotly.

'You're right, she wasn't,' Garrett drawled harshly. 'As long as there was enough there for her to spend on clothes and lavish parties!'

'Amanda was not mercenary!'

'She had no need to be,' Garrett bit out harshly. 'Anything she wanted she could have. What she wanted most of all was the Kingham name!'

'For your son!' Sarah reminded him heatedly.

Fury darkened his eyes before it was quickly brought under control, and Garrett gave a deep sigh. 'Can't you accept me as I am now, that I want you, and forget that I was once married to Amanda?'

'No!' she scorned.

'You will, Sarah,' he told her evenly. 'I promise you, you will.'

She felt hot and irritable once he had gone, despite the fact that the house was very cool. The *only* time she forgot who Garrett was was when he held her in his arms; she would just have to try and make sure she stayed *out* of them. With him equally determined to see her *in* them, that was proving a little difficult.

She had showered and changed out of the linen dress into a cotton one of pale lemon when her bedroom door burst open after the briefest of knocks. Her angry frown turned to a pleased smile as Jason came bounding into the room.

'Sarah!' He picked her up and swung her round the room, hugging her after putting her back down on the floor.

They had all got on well together during Jason's stay with them in England, and he was openly affectionate with her father, but this was the first time he had shown her the same spontaneity. She hugged him back, blinking back the tears.

His youthful face was alight with enthusiasm as he released her. 'This last week just dragged,' he told her melodramatically. 'And then Grand-father, Uncle Jonathan and Aunt Shelley had to arrive yesterday.' He grimaced his feelings about that. 'Which meant I wasn't able to come with Dad to meet you both today. And I'd planned on meeting you. I was going to show you the Chinese Theatre, Hollywood, Beverly Hills——'

'As instructed, your father did all that,' she

smiled. 'Your grandfather loved it.'

'But not you,' he guessed ruefully. 'It's all a bit glitzy, isn't it?'

'Just a bit,' she nodded. 'But then it wouldn't be Hollywood if it weren't.'

'I guess not.' Jason cheered up. 'Are you ready to go and meet the family now? I know,' he laughed as she wasn't quick enough to hide the fact that she wasn't looking forward to it, and doubted she would ever be 'ready'. 'Do you want to know how I always handle meeting Grandfather?'

Grandfather, not the affectionate Grandad that he called her father. If his grandson could still be in awe of him after knowing him all his life, what chance did she have, the sister of the woman William Kingham had openly disapproved of as a wife for his youngest son. 'How?' she prompted interestedly.

'I always try to think of the fact that he must once have been a baby in diapers,' Jason grinned.

She remembered that Amanda had described her father-in-law as cold and rigidly settled on what he considered was right and what was wrong. 'Is that possible?' Sarah derided.

Jason's grin widened. 'It is a little difficult, but if you just try and imagine him in the diaper . . .!'

She put her arm through the crook of his, 'Isn't all this just a little disrespectful?' she chided.

Jason shrugged. 'I was only telling you what I do; you don't have to follow my advice.'

But as she was introduced to William Kingham,

a tall man with iron-grey hair and bearing a striking physical resemblence to his youngest son, the resentment emanating from him unmistakable in the tight-lipped smile and cold hazel eyes, Sarah knew she was going to need all the help she could get. Imagining this tall imposing man as a baby in a nappy certainly had the effect of making her smile a natural one.

Her hand was taken in the limpest of handshakes, even William Kingham's hand being cold and disapproving, while hers felt warm and slightly damp.

Garrett was already in the pool with a beautiful blonde woman she assumed had to be Shelley Kingham, and her father was sitting at a table beneath a brightly coloured umbrella with a blonde-haired man who, if anything, was more classically handsome than Garrett, his smile warm and charming as he concentrated on the man seated opposite him to the exclusion of all else. Sarah didn't need the process of elimination, nor his resemblance to Garrett, to tell her this was Jonathan Kingham; he had the natural charm of a politician.

Her gaze returned reluctantly to the man standing in front of her. 'It's nice to meet you, Senator Kingham,' she told him smoothly.

He nodded. 'You're very much like your sister,' he bit out abruptly.

Her smile faltered slightly, and she frowned as Jason, standing just behind his grandfather now, deliberately attracted her attention. The pointed wink he gave her gave her smile a more natural glow, and she turned away before his gestures made her laugh outright.

Her gaze was as cool as William Kingham's as she turned back to him. 'I believe so,' she drawled challengingly.

William Kingham continued to look at her for several more hostile minutes before giving an abrupt inclination of his head and turning away.

'Whew!' Sarah gave Jason a telling look as he rejoined her. 'If your Uncle Jonathan is as unwelcoming as that I need a breather before you introduce me to him!' She sighed.

Jason grinned. 'Don't worry, Uncle Jonathan is one of the new school of politicians; no matter what happens he's always gracious and charming. But if in doubt, the diaper works on him too,' he added confidingly.

Their shared laughter attracted the attention of the two sitting beneath the umbrella, and Sarah felt a jolt of awareness as brilliant green eyes looked at her warmly. It wasn't at all difficult to see how Jonathan Kingham secured his votes; he just had to smile and both males and females would be drawn to his open honesty.

It was impossible not to return his smile, and she was barely conscious of moving towards him, but suddenly found herself standing beside him as he stood up to greet her, her hand held firmly in his, and for just the right amount of time. He was perfect: tall, blond, tanned, with a genuinely warm smile, even his hand feeling perfect, warm and dry.

'I've been looking forward to meeting you,' he told her gruffly.

She couldn't honestly say the same thing about this family, but Jonathan Kingham could quite easily change her mind.

'Would you care for some iced lemonade?' he offered, pouring her some and holding up the glass for her to take.

Sarah drank obediently, all the time aware of being in the presence of someone charmingly manipulative, a combination it was hard to resist.

He took the empty glass from her unresisting fingers and placed it on the table behind him. 'And now how about a walk on the beach to blow away the cobwebs of travelling?'

Jason was sitting with her father now, William Kingham was still standing beside the house looking at her with sharply disapproving hazel-coloured eyes, and Garrett seemed unaware of her presence at all as yet as he and Shelley still cavorted in the pool. It had been a difficult week, a long day, and a walk along the beach with someone who didn't try to deliberately antagonise her sounded very tempting just now. Garrett certainly wouldn't even notice her absence, she thought unreasonably.

'A walk sounds nice,' she accepted with a smile at the gold-haired Jonathan Kingham. 'Unless I would be taking you away from something—or someone.' She added the last uncertainly, not sure how Shelley Kingham would react to seeing her husband walk off with a relative stranger.

Jonathan's smile widened. 'Shelley and I have been married twenty-one years,' he joked. 'I think by now I can safely assume they're just friends. But even so, I doubt either of them will realise we've gone anywhere.'

As she and Jonathan circled the pool she was aware of Garrett laughing in a light-hearted way she had never heard before, the two in the pool raising a hand of greeting to them before Sarah and Jonathan descended the steps that led down on to the beach, Sarah's frown owing nothing to the concentration the steepness of the steps took. Garrett had looked younger to her somehow just now, his hair slicked back over his head, his body deeply muscled and tanned, a tenderness to his expression as he looked at the woman at his side.

'Garrett told us you're a teacher,' Jonathan remarked as they strolled along together on the golden sand, the ocean deeply blue.

'I try,' she nodded.

'Jason thinks you're pretty wonderful too,' he smiled warmly.

'Does he?' She smiled her pleasure, although that 'too' unnerved her a little. Had Garrett told his brother of his attraction to her? It didn't sound like the reserved man she had come to know, but then she had no idea how close the brothers were. 'That's nice to know,' she added lightly.

'Garrett seems very——' He broke off, frowning. 'Has anyone told you how much like——'

'Amanda I am,' Sarah finished abruptly. 'It has been mentioned, yes.'

'By Garrett?' He looked at her consideringly.

'Jason, actually. And your father just now.' She stopped to watch the crash of the waves against the sand. 'But Garrett thinks so too.'

Jonathan stood beside her, his hands thrust into his trouser pockets, casually fitted brown trousers that gave no indication of their tailored expensiveness. 'It's difficult to know what Garrett is thinking these days,' he sighed.

Sarah stiffened, giving him a frowning look, turning away again as she saw the speculative gleam in those bright green eyes. She had been wrong about this man; he might hide his disapproval behind charm, but he was just as much of a shark as the rest of the Kingham men! 'I can assure you that I have no designs on your baby brother,' she snapped.

Jonathan gave a soft laugh. 'Garrett is a law unto himself, he always has been, and I'm afraid what *you* want won't come into it!'

Her cheeks were flushed. 'My father and I are here because of Jason, no other reason!'

'Sarah—I hope I can call you that,' he added smoothly. 'I was just trying to offer you a little support,' he told her sincerely. 'I'm afraid our father can be a bastard when he doesn't approve of something, and——'

'He doesn't approve of Garrett and me,' she finished tautly; and she had thought this would just be a pleasant walk away from all the tension at

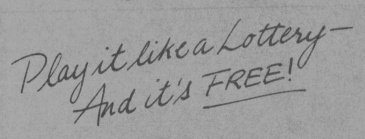

```
* * * * * * * * * * * * * * * * * * * * * * * * *
*   You may have already won a lifetime of cash    *
*   payments totaling up to $1,000,000.00!         *
*   Play our Sweepstakes Game -- Here's how...     *
* * * * * * * * * * * * * * * * * * * * * * * * *
```

On each of the first three tickets (numbered 1 to 3)
there is a <u>silver area</u>. Using an eraser, rub off the
silver box to reveal how much each ticket could be worth—
you must return the <u>entire</u> card to be eligible.

   Each of the first three tickets also has a unique
Sweepstakes number. When you return your game card,
we'll check to see if your Sweepstakes numbers match any
of the winning numbers already selected by our computer.
If so, you'll win the amount shown under the rub-off
area on that ticket. See official rules in back of this
book for details.

   Harlequin also invites you to participate in a
new Sampling Project by accepting one or more totally
FREE books! To request your free book(s), please rub off
the area below the question mark on ticket 4 to reveal
how many free books you will receive.

   When you receive your free book(s), we hope you'll
enjoy them and want to see more. So unless we hear from
you, a month later we'll send you 8 additional novels.
Each book is yours to keep for only $2.24 each -- 26¢
less per book than what you pay in stores -- plus 89¢
shipping and handling per shipment -- and of course,
you may cancel any time.

Plus—you get a FREE MYSTERY GIFT!

If you return your game card with <u>all four silver
areas</u> rubbed off, you will also receive a FREE Mystery
Gift. It's your <u>immediate reward</u> for playing our
Sweepstakes Game <u>and</u> sampling your free book(s).

P.S.

The first set of one or more books is FREE. So rub off
the box on ticket 4 and return entire sheet of tickets!

the house! 'I just told you, there's no relationship between us to disapprove of!'

Jonathan sighed, his hands clasping her arms just above the wrists. 'Please don't be offended by anything that I've said——'

'Offended?' She pulled away from him, her eyes flashing deeply blue. 'Why should I be offended just because my host's brother has warned me off him only minutes after my arrival!'

'My God, you *are* like Amanda . . .!' He looked at her admiringly.

'Enough to be able to tell you that even if Garrett and I *were* involved it would be none of your business! Now, if you will excuse me——' She came to an abrupt halt as she turned to find Garrett standing a short distance away from them looking like a Greek god, tall and golden, his masculinity left in no doubt in the clinging black swim-trunks.

His narrowed gaze took in the flush to her cheeks and the mutinous expression in her eyes before moving coldly on to his brother. 'Shelley would like you to join her now,' he bit out evenly.

Jonathan nodded. 'I'll go to her. Sarah,' he looked at her tight-lipped face frowningly, 'I didn't mean to offend you,' he told her softly before striding off towards the house.

Sarah looked at Garrett defiantly, expecting criticism for the outburst he must surely have heard, her eyes widening as it didn't come.

'You looked as if you needed rescuing,' he remarked huskily, standing beside her now.

Her breath left her body in a relieved sigh. 'I get the feeling this is going to be far from a relaxing holiday for me!'

His eyes narrowed. 'If anyone has said anything to hurt you I'll——'

'Your father is angry because I look so much like Amanda, and your brother seemed pleased that I do!' she snapped.

Garrett shook his head. 'They see only what they want to see; to me you're just Sarah.'

She shouldn't have felt pleased, but she did. 'Dad seems happy here, at least.'

Garrett nodded, smiling. 'He and Jason have already gone off in search of a chessboard!'

She felt the tension of the last half-hour leaving her, and started to relax, something she had never thought she could do around this man. But of the three Kingham men he was turning out to be the least formidable and the most honest. It would be just her luck if Shelley Kingham turned out to be unwelcoming as the two older Kingham men!

'I wanted to come to your room for you earlier,' Garrett told her gruffly. 'But Jason insisted he wanted to be the one to get you.'

It was a mistake *ever* to relax around this man! 'I was pleased to see him again,' she said stiffly.

Garrett drew in a ragged breath. 'Is it so difficult to admit you're pleased to see *me* again too?' he groaned, his eyes dark. 'I've thought of nothing and no one but you this last week; can't you tell me you thought of me a little too?'

Thought of him a *little*? She hadn't been able to

think of anything else! He had left that night a week ago after telling her they would one day make love, openly and unashamedly, that they had something special between them, and he had shaken up all her former ideas of her own sensuality. How could she *not* have thought about him, and the things just being with him did to her?

She had started dating at fifteen, had dated often and with various boys until she had met David when she was nineteen and at college, had married him when she was barely twenty. He hadn't even been her first steady boyfriend, but she had found no difficulty in rebuffing a physical relationship with him before their marriage as she had with those other boys, a physical relationship David thought they should have.

He hadn't accepted her refusals gracefully, but he had accepted them, and as the months passed and he began to talk in anticipation of their wedding night it became obvious how much he was relying on that to take the sting out of all the refusals he had so far received from her. On their wedding night she had told herself that her lack of response had been *because* she felt so much pressure from David. But as the days, weeks and finally months passed, and she still hadn't been able to give him the response he wanted, it had become something that neither of them could live with.

Because David had wanted it that way, and because she hadn't wanted to hurt him any more than she already had, the two of them had been divorced, when really their marriage could have been annulled because of non-consummation!

David had wanted her so much, had tried so hard, in so many ways, to arouse her, but when he failed time and time again, instead of taking her angrily as so many men would have done, he had turned away from her in disgust.

She was twenty-six years old, had been married, but was still a virgin because her husband hadn't been able to arouse desire in her. And yet if Garrett asked her to she knew she would lie down with him on the sand now and give herself to him, as he had once claimed in England that she would!

CHAPTER SIX

FRIGID, David had called her angrily at the end of their traumatic marriage, and until Garrett came back into her life she had believed him. Now she knew she was far from that, and she was just as frightened of her fevered reaction to Garrett as she had been of her coldness in David's arms.

'I cursed your arrogance and damned your machinations, so I suppose I must have thought of you,' she bit out coldly.

'Oh, Sarah.' He shook his head, lines of strain beside his eyes. 'I'm being completely honest with you, why can't you be the same way with me?'

She raised dark brows. 'I thought I was.'

Garrett sighed heavily. 'Is it so wrong to admit you find me attractive?'

'Yes, damn you, it is!' Her eyes flashed. 'It's disloyal to Amanda.'

He drew in a ragged breath, his hand falling away from her arm. 'Amanda *died* years ago! You were still a child, and our marriage was in ruins. It would only be disloyal to Amanda if she were *alive* and we felt this way about each other.'

'I——'

'Don't kid yourself we wouldn't feel this way if she were alive,' he rasped. 'We might not do anything about it in those circumstances, but the awareness would still be there! There's always been something between us, but you were still a child and I didn't recognise it for attraction until ten days ago.'

She had known, had always known. She turned abruptly away. 'Leave me alone, Garrett. Just leave me alone!'

'I can't.' He shook his head wearily. 'I can't even promise to give you time to get used to the idea before I come to you.' His eyes were pained. 'I've had sex with other women over the last ten years, but just touching you gives me more satisfaction than I knew with any of them. I think—I'll die a little when I finally make love to you!'

'No!' Sarah was very white, the chill of her body having nothing to do with the temperature of the day.

'Yes.' It was a hoarse groan of defeat.

She didn't deny it this time, she just turned and ran, breathing hard in the heat of the day before she even reached the steps up to the house, glancing back across the beach as she reached the top of those steps. Garrett stood exactly where she had left him, silently watching her.

She was completely unprepared for the shock that greeted her as she walked beside the pool. Shelley Kingham was out of the water now, sitting with the four men in the shade of an umbrella, her beautiful face aglow with happiness. And she was in a wheelchair.

Her body was perfectly formed in the black

bikini, tall and shapely, and yet those beautifully
long legs were immobile on the foot-rests that
supported them.

Amanda had never mentioned in any of her
letters that her sister-in-law was confined to a
wheelchair, and perhaps she hadn't considered it
important, but Sarah wished she had been pre-
warned, for she could have reacted embarrassingly
if she hadn't had time to take in the other woman's
incapacity before any of them became aware of her
presence.

She gave a start of surprise as she felt the
warmth of Garrett's hand against her spine, her
bare skin feeling an instant warmth beneath his
touch. She turned to look at him uncertainly.

His expression was gentle. 'No matter how
many arguments we have it's not going to change
how I feel about you.'

'But——'

'Come on, I'll introduce you to Shelley,' he
invited huskily. 'Next to Jason she is by far the
nicest member of my family,' he added ruefully.

Shelley proved to be exactly that, warm and
welcoming, although there was a slight reserve to
her manner that Sarah put down to the awkwardness of the situation. William Kingham sat slightly
apart from the rest of them, obviously deeply
disapproving of her presence here at all.

After being in Shelley's company for half an
hour Sarah realised exactly why Amanda had
never thought to mention the other woman was in
a wheelchair; after being with her only that short a

time she forgot all about the wheelchair herself! In her late thirties, Shelley had a vivacity that drew one's attention to the glowing beauty of her face and the mischief in her dark grey eyes, rather than to the fact that she couldn't get up and walk.

Jonathan was more relaxed in his wife's company too, and by the time Sarah returned to her room to rest before dinner she felt a little more at ease, less like a resented outsider.

The coolness she had noticed in the lounge was carried over into the bedrooms, and after sitting out in the heat of the afternoon it was delicious to undress and then curl up to sleep beneath the cool sheets. On the occasions Amanda had flown home to visit them she had complained of jet-lag, and now that Sarah was experiencing it first-hand she realised just how awful it made you feel.

She was in that twilight state between wakefulness and sleep, her body protesting at the need for sleep when the sun was still shining outside, even though it craved the rest, when she saw the shadowy figure beside her bed. Golden-blond hair glistened in the light peeping behind the curtains, and a hand moved to gently caress the softness of her cheek.

'Garrett ...!' she murmured sleepily, not knowing if she were alarmed or aroused by his intrusion into her bedroom.

'Go to sleep,' he told her gruffly.

Sarah sighed her disappointment as she watched the shadowy figure move silently to the door, leaving as quietly as he had arrived.

A maid came in to wake her with a tray of tea shortly before six, and as the memory of Garrett's visit came back to her she wondered if it had all been a dream. If it had then her heated response was her secret, but if Garrett had really come in here ...!

How was she going to go on telling Garrett she didn't want him after that? She blushed as she remembered the way her body had arched for the knowing caress of his hand, knew the way she had groaned his name had been an open invitation.

Maybe she could cry off eating dinner with the rest of the family with the excuse that she had a headache? She certainly did have a headache, her sleep having been deep and unrestful, but she was also hungry, and to ask for a tray in her room would look a little odd when she was supposed to be feeling ill. Besides, she couldn't give Garrett the satisfaction of knowing he had her on the run. There was always the possibility that his being here *had* been a dream, but if he had been here in her bedroom then he had no right to have been, and if he referred to it she would tell him so, in no uncertain terms!

Unfortunately, the first person she saw when she walked into the lounge was William Kingham!

She instantly did a mental review of her appearance—the long halter-necked dress of pure white was a perfect foil for her long dark hair and tanned skin, her make-up faultless when she left her room mere seconds ago. And yet under this man's critical gaze she felt under-dressed and over-painted.

'Senator Kingham,' she greeted politely, sitting down to wait for the others to join them; sometimes punctuality could be a burden, she was learning. But years of being on time for classes, both as a student and a teacher, meant that she couldn't bring herself to be late for anything; Garrett had said seven o'clock, and it was that now. Obviously only the elder Senator and herself had felt the need to keep to that time.

'Miss Harvey,' he greeted as stiltedly, standing stiffly across the room from her.

She looked at him coolly. 'Didn't Garrett tell you, my married name is Croft.' She chastised herself for the inward thrill of satisfaction she felt at startling him out of his cold condescension, his eyes narrowing questioningly.

'Garrett didn't tell us you have a husband,' he finally rasped.

'Oh, I don't,' she told him lightly. 'Not any more.'

'You're very young to have been married and divorced.' He looked at her speculatively.

Sarah met his gaze steadily. 'We tend to marry young in my family.'

His mouth tightened with contempt. 'I'm well aware of that fact. It would seem you also have a tendency to discard your husbands as soon as the honeymoon is over!'

Sarah bristled angrily. 'You know absolutely nothing about my marriage——'

'How beautiful you look, darling,' Garrett told her huskily as he entered the room, wearing a white dinner jacket and black trousers, although his father was dressed in a more formal black evening suit. He bent to kiss Sarah on the tightness of her lips, his narrowed gaze moving from Sarah's flushed face to his father's coldly set one. 'Doesn't she, Father?' he prompted in a hard voice as he sat down beside Sarah, his arm casually about her shoulders.

William Kingham's gaze flickered over her dispassionately. 'Beauty doesn't seem to be one of the things the Harvey women lack,' he bit out contemptuously.

'You——'

'You really do look lovely, sweetheart.' Garrett turned to kiss the bareness of her shoulder, a warning look in his eyes as she would have openly rejected the familiarity of the caress.

She could see how angry his behaviour was making his father, and she couldn't help but feel shocked by this open display of possession herself. She knew he had said he refused to be clandestine where she was concerned, but this . . .!

'Excuse me,' his father rasped harshly. 'I'll come back when you've finished fondling your mistress!' He strode from the room, his back ramrod-straight, disgust in every line of his body.

Sarah gave a choked sob, all the tension leaving her body as she dropped back against the sofa, her face deathly white.

'I'm sorry,' Garrett told her raggedly, searching her face concernedly.

'What did you expect?' she groaned, her eyes
tear-bright. 'Your father despises me and my
family, and you were openly flaunting me in his
face.' She trembled in reaction to the awful scene.

He touched her cheek gently. 'Maybe I
shouldn't have put you through that, but I had to
show him that you're important to me, and that I
expect him to treat you with a certain amount of
respect, when you're with me or alone—something he wasn't doing when I came in,' he added
grimly.

Her mouth tightened as she remembered what
William Kingham had said to her. 'You expect
him to respect me?' she scorned. 'The woman he
now thinks is having an affair with her sister's
husband!'

'Sarah, we've been through this before; I've
been alone for ten years,' he reasoned. 'We aren't
having an affair, and I'm not *anyone's* husband.'

She shook her head. 'Your father will never see
it that way.'

'Do you think I give a damn what he thinks?' he
dismissed hardly. '*You're* what's important to me,
Sarah. Sarah!' he groaned raggedly, tilting her
chin so that her lips quivered invitingly beneath
his. 'God, how I need you!'

She needed him too at that moment, raw as she
was from William Kingham's contempt of her.

It was a gentle kiss, their lips moving together in
slow exploration, nothing demanding, just pure
enjoyment of the senses, Sarah's hand resting

against Garrett's chest as he held her within the cradle of his arms.

'Maybe we're a little early for dinner—or whatever.'

Sarah's sensual lethargy was such that for a brief moment her father's teasing comment didn't penetrate the heady excitement she had drifted into without too much persuasion. And then she realised where they were, and she straightened away from Garrett to find they had quite an audience—Jonathan and Shelley just behind her father and Jason.

Colour instantly darkened her cheeks. 'I—we——' She looked at Garrett in desperation.

His answer was to look at them all challengingly, his arm still firmly about her shoulders, his fingers lightly caressing her bare flesh. 'Would anyone like a drink before dinner?' he drawled lightly.

Sarah looked at her father searchingly, looking for some sign of reproach. He seemed surprised, but certainly not disapproving. Probably he was *too* surprised to be that yet! she thought with a groan.

'I would,' she requested shakily. 'A large brandy!'

The moment of awkwardness was covered by Garrett standing up to pour everyone a drink, Shelley moving forward to engage Sarah in conversation about a book she had recently read and which Sarah found she had read too. By the time William Kingham strode back into the room conversation was flowing easily, although Sarah was very much aware of the fact that Jason watched her as if he had never seen her before. If she had harmed her relationship with him——

But what of her relationship with Garrett? A moment of weakness and they had as good as made a public declaration of their feelings for each other, to their families at least! Garrett might be happy with that, but she wasn't, she *wasn't*.

Dinner couldn't be over quickly enough for her, and she excused her lack of appetite as tiredness because of the long flight, following her father to his bedroom when he excused himself just after the meal.

'Don't look so stricken, Sarah,' he chided as she looked at him appealingly. 'There's no shame in being attracted to the man. Heaven knows he's a handsome devil!' He took off his dinner jacket wearily and hung it up in the wardrobe.

'He was Amanda's husband,' she reminded him self-disgustedly.

'A very long time ago,' her father dismissed gently. 'I'm glad you've found someone else at last, I've been worried about you since you and David separated.'

Sarah had always been too embarrassed to discuss the problems she and David had had with her father, had even tried going out with other men after she and David were divorced, only to find she was just as cold with them. Finally she had stopped dating altogether, tired of fighting off advances that meant absolutely nothing to her.

But she hadn't realised that her lack of interest in another relationship had worried her father.

'But Garrett?' she pointed out painfully.

'Why not?' he shrugged, sitting down tiredly on the side of his bed.

'You know why,' she sighed.

'Sarah, Garrett didn't make Amanda pregnant all on his own; she was there too, a willing participant.' He shook his head. 'She could have stopped him making love to her if she had wanted to; a woman can usually stop a man. I know damn well he didn't rape her!'

And she had evidence herself of the sort of control Garrett could exert over his emotions, able to draw back and be sensible for them both, when she had begged him to take her. But he might not have had the same control at twenty-three!

'I don't want to be attracted to him,' she told her father determinedly.

His eyes twinkled deeply blue. 'One thing I've always known about Garrett; when he wants something he usually gets it,' he drawled.

'I'm not a film-script or a car, Dad,' she protested indignantly.

'No,' he acknowledged seriously. 'I think you're much more important to Garrett than either of those things could ever be. And, considering how his family would obviously feel about that, I admire him for being so honest about it.'

She frowned. 'You sound as if you actually like him!'

He shrugged again. 'I've never *disliked* him, only what he and Amanda did to each other and Jason. They were completely wrong for each other from the start, but I respect them for at least trying to make a success of their marriage.'

'He made Amanda so unhappy——'

'I'm sure that worked both ways,' he sighed. 'Amanda could be very selfish and wilful——'

'Dad!'

'Oh, I know you've built your sister up to be some sort of paragon over the years, someone who could do no wrong, but Amanda was wild, and very often selfish; you were just too young to see and realise that,' he added gently. 'Your mother and I feared for her when she decided to come here, but she was eighteen and there wasn't a thing we could do to stop her. Asking certainly never worked! When she came home six months later, married, and carrying Garrett's child, our worst fears were realised.'

'He may not have forced her, but he seduced her——'

'No, Sarah, he didn't, and I'm not going to let you tell yourself that lie so that you can avoid what *you* feel for him. At eighteen Amanda was more sophisticated than you are now,' he insisted. 'In fact, I'm sure Garrett was far from her first lover. She certainly knew that she didn't have to marry Garrett just because she was pregnant, knew that your mother and I would help support her for as long as she needed us.' He leant forward to clasp Sarah's hand. 'You have to realise that Amanda *wanted* to marry Garrett and have his child, why I don't know, because she certainly never loved him.' He sighed. 'You mustn't give up your own chance at happiness because of what happened with Amanda.'

'Garrett could never make me happy,' she denied with vehemence.

Her father gave a sad smile. 'Heaven and hell can sometimes be so close together.'

Garrett had shown her *both* heaven and hell; heaven when she was in his arms, hell when she was out of them!

She swallowed hard. 'I've always despised women who claim to be confused all the time, but I am confused about your attitude!'

He shook his head. 'It isn't so difficult to understand; I just want you to be with the person who can make you happy.'

And he seemed convinced that Garrett was the man who could be that person, Sarah realised as she slowly went back to her bedroom.

But she wasn't convinced at all; she still harboured too much resentment towards him to accept meekly the relationship he wanted with her. And she had a feeling Jason was even more confused and hurt by what was going on than she was.

Going in search of him, and learning from one of the maids clearing away for the evening that Jason had already gone to bed, Sarah made her way back to her own bedroom, her heart skipping a beat as she saw Garrett coming down the corridor towards her.

Pleasure blazed in his eyes as his gaze rested on her. 'Looking for me?' he encouraged throatily.

She blushed deeply red. 'Of course not,' she snapped uncomfortably.

His eyes dulled at her answer, frowning darkly. 'Who, then?'

'Jason,' she sighed. 'He barely spoke to me after he saw the two of us together earlier. I wanted to——'

'Talk to him,' Garrett finished, nodding his understanding. 'I've just left him. He understands.'

'Understands what?' She raised dark brows.

'That, although we didn't ask for it, or go looking for it, we're attracted to each other!' Garrett rasped harshly.

Sarah drew in a ragged breath. 'You told him that?' she demanded indignantly.

Garrett's eyes narrowed, his stance one of challenge. 'Yes.'

'You had no right!' she snapped, her body tense. 'I wanted——'

'I'm getting a little tired of fighting you, even when you know I'm right.' He gave a harsh sigh.

'You aren't right! You—what do you think you're doing?' She gasped as her wrist was clasped and he pulled her along beside him.

His expression was grim. 'Taking you to my bedroom where I can——'

'You—are—not!' She came to an abrupt halt despite the pain she inflicted to her wrist, breathing hard, her eyes stormy.

He turned to her with narrowed eyes as she refused to budge from that spot despite his insistent tugging. 'Okay,' he finally bit out gratingly, pushing open a door beside him. 'If that's the way you want it!' He pulled her into the room with him.

Sarah had expected a guest bedroom, or at least a bathroom, but instead she found herself in a linen cupboard!

Garrett looked about them ruefully, the light to the small room having come on automatically when he opened the door. As linen cupboards went it was quite a large room, shelves of clean towels and sheets either side of them, having that same faintly floral smell Sarah had noticed on her sheets as she rested this afternoon.

Remembering that rest reminded her of Garrett's intrusion to her room as she lay there trying to sleep, and she took refuge in her anger as the door closed behind them and they were left in complete darkness. 'I hope you don't subject all your female guests to the lack of privacy that I've suffered since I arrived!' she snapped.

His lips travelled the length of her creamy throat. 'I found you in the corridor, Sarah——'

'I'm not talking about now, I meant this afternoon.' She remained stiff in his arms. 'I don't appreciate the fact that in future the only way to stop you creeping into my bedroom and touching me while I'm trying to sleep is to lock my door!' The bite of his teeth against her throat was too painful to be playful, and Sarah drew back angrily.

Garrett's warm breath caressed her face. 'You didn't like it?'

'It was despicable!' Luckily the darkness hid the blush to her cheeks.

He sighed. 'Then it won't happen again,' he promised her.

She drew back as far as he would let her. 'You said that too easily——'

'I promised, Sarah,' he rasped. 'Now please, darling, kiss me before I go completely insane!'

Her legs went weak at his hoarse pleading, their lips meeting with unerring accuracy, Sarah's arms going up about his neck as she gave a groan of surrender.

She didn't know why she even tried to fight this man, she groaned inwardly, as the heat filled her body and the halter-neck of her gown slid caressingly down her body to her hips, sensual hands instantly taking its place against her heated flesh.

CHAPTER SEVEN

SARAH'S body pulsed and tensed, Garrett's mouth claiming hers even as his hands cupped her bared breasts, plucking at the sleeping nipples until they pulsed too, her back arching in a silent plea.

Her head was thrown back, her hands resting on Garrett's shoulders for support as he cupped her breasts for his delectation, kissing first one and then the other, her whimpers of need answered as his warm breath caressed her.

Her pulse thundered, her hands clutched in the silky softness of his hair as she drew his mouth to her. He drank his fill, returning again and again to the sustenance he drew from her, his breathing harshly erratic.

Sarah could only groan weakly as he pushed the dress down over her thighs to fall to the ground at her feet, a thin wisp of satin and lace her only piece of clothing now, and warmth spreading over her whole body as one of his hands closed over her possessively.

'Sarah, we can't make love here,' he gasped wildly. 'You——'

'Don't stop,' she sobbed, feeling herself on the edge of a wondrous discovery, the warmth in her body becoming unbearable. 'Oh God, Garrett, don't stop!' She clung to him.

'Dear God, I wish I could see you——'

'You don't need to see me,' she told him breathlessly. 'Touch me. *Feel*!'

Her legs gave way completely as his hand moved surely beneath the lace to touch her moistness, and the two of them sank to the floor, the carpet there softening their fall, Garrett's mouth never leaving hers as he slowly caressed her.

She wasn't able to control the tiny explosions of her body, knowing she had almost reached the most beautiful ache in the world, a heat that would engulf her body until she felt as if she had climbed a mountain and conquered.

Garrett kissed her languidly, soothingly, calming her, the moistness of his mouth easing the ache from her breasts before he moved down to kiss her through the satin, dampening their desire to hold her in his arms.

Her breasts were tender from his ministrations, even as she could feel his fully clothed body against hers. She turned to him in the darkness. 'But we haven't—we haven't——'

'It's all right, my Sarah.' He kissed her slowly. 'I only wanted to give you a little pleasure.'

'But——'

'Darling, I've never known anything as beautiful as having you in my arms,' he assured her huskily, still caressing in slow soothing moments that calmed her need for complete release. 'But I can't take you here.'

A blush of mortification darkened her cheeks. 'But I didn't even touch you——'

'The pleasure is in the giving, Sarah,' he groaned. 'Feeling the way you caught fire made me feel complete for the first time in my life.'

'But we haven't——'

'And we aren't going to either.' He gently helped her on with her dress, doing up the button at her nape himself. 'You're like a beautiful present I'm tormenting myself with, opening it a little at a time to prolong the pleasure I know will eventually come.'

'I wouldn't have stopped you——'

'I know that.' He was smiling at her tenderly as he opened the door for her and the light automatically came back on, his eyes dark with pleasure as he paused to kiss her once more. 'In a linen closet, no less,' he teased, his arm about her waist as he accompanied her back to her bedroom.

Sarah was too dazed to care about their surroundings; she knew that, like her, Garrett was too happy that she had surrendered to him to care *where* it had happened. She felt like a woman as she never had before, knew that she could reach that pinnacle with Garrett, had almost done so. And although she was still a virgin she knew that it would only be a matter of time before Garrett made her his completely. When Garrett was the only man ever to give her physical pleasure, it seemed only right that he should be the one to take her virginity.

She slept heavily, waking late the next day, hurrying out of bed, eager to see Garrett again, to assure herself that the magic of the previous night had really happened and not just been a dream. If it had she had never had a dream like that one before!

She felt so wonderfully alive, the tingling of her body not altogether due to the hot spray of the shower pelting down on her. She wanted Garrett to make love to her, knew desire now and craved it.

Her disappointment was acute when she joined Shelley on the patio and the other woman told her that Garrett had had to go to the studio today, although she cheered up a little when Shelley told her Garrett had left the message for her that he would be back as soon as he could get away.

'You love him, don't you?' Shelley said gently at the radiant smile on Sarah's face.

She sobered instantly, sipping at the freshly brewed coffee to calm her nerves. 'Until he came to see us eleven days ago I barely knew him.' She avoided voicing the emotions that were still such a surprise to her.

Shelley smiled. 'I've known Garrett twenty-two years, and I've never seen him as happy as he was this morning!'

Pleasure brightened her eyes. 'Really?'

'Really.' The other woman's smile warmed.

Sarah frowned. 'Aren't you going to tell me how much like Amanda I am, and how wrong I am for Garrett, like the rest of the family?'

'You're nothing at all like Amanda,' Shelley denied tautly. 'I knew that five minutes after meeting you.'

Sarah's frown deepened as she recalled that that

was how long it had taken for the other woman's reserve to drop. 'Didn't you and Amanda get on together?' she probed gently.

It seemed to her that Shelley's smile was more than a little forced now. 'Why shouldn't we have done?' she dismissed.

She didn't know. To her Amanda had always appeared bright and beautiful, Jason remembered her as 'the beautiful woman who brought him presents', Garrett said she had been 'mercenary', and her father called her 'wilful and selfish'; what had she been to Shelley Kingham? It didn't sound as if any of them were talking about the same person.

'I don't remember Amanda very well now,' Sarah sighed regretfully. 'But it seems to me that she was different things to different people.' She shrugged. 'I wondered what she was to you?'

'Well, we weren't friends, if that's what you mean,' Shelley told her abruptly.

That *did* explain the reserve she had sensed in this woman yesterday until she had realised she was nothing like Amanda! 'None of Garrett's family seems to have liked my sister,' she said ruefully.

'I shouldn't let it bother you; it certainly didn't worry Amanda,' Shelley told her drily.

Sarah gave a pained frown. 'Why is it that everyone blames her for marrying Garrett rather than the other way around?'

'No one *blames* her for marrying him,' Shelley sighed. 'She just did little to endear herself after they were married.'

In the face of all this open resentment Sarah wasn't sure she would be feeling all that friendly either!

But she thought it best to change the subject, encouraging Shelley to talk about the help she gave her husband in his demanding career. She sounded like the organiser behind the team.

She was still sitting with Shelley when lunchtime came around. Garrett was still out, and the other four men had driven into town before she was up, whether separately or together she wasn't sure. William Kingham didn't harbour the same resentment towards her father that he did towards her, and she knew it was because she reminded him too much of Amanda.

Garrett didn't join them for lunch, but the others arrived back just before the meal was about to be served. Her father looked relaxed and less tired today, Jonathan was his usual charming self, and even William Kingham didn't scowl at her enough to sour the food before it reached her mouth!

But it was to Jason Sarah looked the most, still uncertain of his reaction to her even though Garrett had assured her the two of them had spoken and Jason understood. He was certainly more relaxed with her today than he had been at dinner last night, but she still sensed a little reserve on his part.

'Could I come with you?' she asked after lunch when he announced he was going surfing.

He looked at her in some surprise. 'If you want to,' he shrugged non-committally.

'I'd like to,' she nodded eagerly, going to her room to get her things.

She was a little disappointed not to find herself alone with him as she had wanted, Jonathan deciding to join them when Shelley and Sarah's father opted for a nap and William Kingham announced he had some work to do. But as Jason and his surfboard immediately disappeared into the water with the other youngsters there once they got down on to the beach she was glad of Jonathan's company, waving to Dennis as he made himself comfortable a short distance up the beach.

Jonathan looked at the other man too. 'I forgot he was there,' he said ruefully.

Sarah turned back. 'I think that's the general idea.' But she still found the other man's presence a little disconcerting. 'No wonder Jason found our waves in England so tame!' she grimaced as Jason easily manoeuvred his board on the crest of one of the highest waves she had ever seen.

Jonathan laughed, sitting back on the sand beside her. 'I sometimes think Jason was born on a surfboard!'

'Do you surf?'

He shook his head. 'There isn't much call for it in Washington,' he derided.

'I meant when you were younger.' She chided his mockery.

He sobered. 'Was I ever young?' he grimaced,

lying back on the sand, his hands behind his head, dark glasses shielding his eyes in the bright sunshine. 'Garrett always thought he was the hard-done-by son, the one searching for his own identity. He didn't stop to consider how difficult it was having your identity, your *life*, already decided for you!'

There was no bitterness in his tone, and she couldn't see the emotion in his eyes, but she did sense resentment in his words.

'I was the elder son,' he continued drily. 'Of course I would go into politics like my father!'

Sarah watched him closely, suddenly still. 'Didn't you want to?'

He sat up, brushing the sand from his arms. 'Strangely enough, I did.' He shrugged. 'It's what I do best.'

'Then why the resentment?' she probed softly.

'Is that the way it sounded?' he frowned. 'I didn't mean it to.' He smiled. 'But it's at moments like this, watching Jason enjoy his youth, that I realise somewhere along the way I missed out on mine, that I've had to live my life by too rigid a code.'

'And Garrett?'

He gave a soft laugh. 'By the time he was seventeen my father was already calling him a disgrace to the family! Of course, that just made him all the more determined to shock our puritan father. For years the newspapers were full of the escapades of the younger son of Senator Kingham!'

She smiled as she imagined Garrett a little older than Jason, deliberately shocking his father to get a reaction. 'I'm sure he enjoyed that,' she mused.

Jonathan grinned, looking years younger. 'It appealed to his sense of humour!'

'And yours?' She looked at him curiously.

He shrugged. 'I often wished I had his daring,' he admitted. 'Instead I was a model student, made the perfect social marriage, and became one of the youngest senators this country has ever known!'

'You've regretted it?' Sarah frowned.

'Occasionally,' he conceded lightly. 'Sometimes the rules can be too strict to live by and be completely happy all the time. The one thing I've never regretted is Shelley; I've loved her from the moment I first saw her.'

She could believe that; she had witnessed the open love the couple had for each other.

'How about you?' Jonathan gave her a sideways glance. 'My father told me you were married.'

'I'll just bet he did—and enjoyed listing my failings,' she said with sarcasm.

Jonathan smiled. 'Once you've known him a while you'll realise he's the way he is because of the love he has for his family.'

'I don't think I'll be around long enough to make that discovery,' she dismissed drily.

He frowned. 'But I thought you and Garrett— you seemed—perhaps I was mistaken,' he excused awkwardly.

He had *thought* that she and Garrett were serious about each other, they had *seemed* to be in love;

she knew that had been what Jonathan Kingham had intended saying as clearly as if he had finished each sentence!

Was Garrett in love with her? He certainly hadn't said that he was, for all of his possessiveness, but then she hadn't told him of her feelings for him either. And even if they were in love she wasn't stupid enough to think Garrett would want to marry her, and how could they go on seeing each other with her living in England and Garrett living here?

'I think perhaps you were,' she told Jonathan gently.

He trailed one finger down the softness of her cheek. 'My brother will be a fool if he lets you get away from him.'

She smiled, colouring slightly at the compliment. 'Aren't we all a little foolish at times?'

'Yes,' he rasped, his expression suddenly closed.

Sarah turned to watch Jason as he surfed into the shore once again. She still hadn't had the opportunity to talk to him, but he had seemed friendly enough on the way down here, so maybe he really did understand about her and Garrett.

She certainly felt as if she knew Jonathan a little better after their talk this afternoon. Maybe it wasn't so easy being the 'golden-spoon' sons of Senator William Kingham after all.

When they got back to the house, Jason challenged her to a race in the pool, and while the others lounged beside the water, her father and Shelley having joined them now, they swam lap after lap up and down the pool.

Finally Sarah laughingly conceded defeat, and got out of the water as, after a triumphant grin in her direction, Jason swam a lap of honour.

The first person Sarah saw as she pulled herself out of the water to sit on the side was Garrett, who took her hands in his as he pulled her to her feet in front of him.

'You have the most beautiful body, clothed or unclothed, that I have ever seen,' he murmured softly, his head bent to hers as he raised her chin and claimed her lips with his own.

'So it's just my body you're after?' she teased shakily when the kiss reluctantly ended.

'Is it?' he murmured softly.

She had been his for the taking last night, and yet he hadn't taken her, despite wanting her very badly. She looked at him with candid blue eyes. 'Maybe it's just *your* body I'm after.'

His tender expression didn't change. 'Is it?' he said again.

Was it? She didn't think so, but at the moment her wanting was all mixed up with the loving. She swallowed hard. 'Garrett, we have to talk about my marriage to David——'

'Because he never gave you the pleasure that I have?'

She looked up at him sharply, finding only indulgent understanding in his expression. 'How did you know that?' she frowned.

'Because you're slightly afraid of what I can make you feel,' he explained gently. 'And it's a fear brought on by inexperience. Don't worry, darling,' he smoothed the frown from her brow, 'you aren't the first married woman never to have reached a climax during lovemaking.'

'It isn't just that——'

'Darling, this conversation, and your proximity, is doing noticeable things to my body!' he groaned.

She could feel his pulsating desire. 'Perhaps you need cooling off?' she queried lightly.

'What—no, Sarah.' He moved back protestingly as he saw the mischievous glint in her eyes. 'Sarah, no—o—o—o,' he cried just before he hit the water, the spray from his inelegant landing going all over the side.

Sarah didn't mind the wetting she got, bursting into laughter as Garrett surfaced spluttering water and promising retribution, his shirt and trousers clinging to him like a second skin.

'Need a little help, Dad?' Jason queried beside her before calmly pushing her into the water beside Garrett.

She had time to hear Garrett's heart-felt 'Thanks, son' before she disappeared beneath the water in a resounding crash, opening her eyes wide as she felt her shoulders grasped and hard lips come down on her own.

They were still kissing as they surfaced, although they drew apart to gasp in huge gulps of air to their starved lungs.

'Enjoying your swim?' she drawled mockingly.

His hair was plastered darkly to his head, the

darker shade of hair on his chest visible through the transparent lemon shirt. 'A cold shower might have been a little less drastic.' He pulled the damp cotton away from his body with a grimace. 'But the swim had the same effect, I can assure you. I missed you today,' he added gruffly, his eyes warm.

'I missed you too,' she admitted huskily, as the two of them trod water side by side. 'I——'

'When the two of you have quite finished making an exhibition of yourselves in front of the servants . . .!'

Green eyes hardened coldly as they left Sarah to move to his father as he stood furiously at the side of the pool. 'I don't have servants, Father, just people who work for me,' he bit out abruptly. 'And if Sarah and I chose to strip off here and now and make love I don't believe it would be any of your business!'

'Have you forgotten you're visible to your son?' Hazel eyes glittered furiously.

Firm hands held Sarah to Garrett's side even though his gaze remained firmly locked with his father's. 'He, at least, has the sense not to try and stop me!'

Garrett's scorn was obviously the last straw as far as his father was concerned. 'You would put that woman before your family?'

Garrett's eyes narrowed. 'Is it going to come to that?'

'I will not stay here and witness your disgusting

behaviour with *that* woman!' his father said disgustedly.

Garrett nodded grimly. 'In that case, I believe you know where the door is.'

His father went completely white. 'Is that your final word on the subject?'

He gave a curt inclination of his head. 'I can assure you I have no intention of staying away from Sarah.'

'Very well,' William Kingham bit out coldly. 'When you come to your senses I will be back in Washington—waiting for your apology!'

'You'll wait in vain,' Garrett muttered roughly as his father strode away.

'Garrett——'

He looked at Sarah with luminous green eyes. 'How would you like to come to my room with me and help me get dry?' he rasped.

She knew he was asking for more than that, that the scene with his father had disturbed him more than he was prepared to show, that he *needed* her. But this was so important to her, she couldn't just be *any* woman who could give him the same time of forgetfulness in her arms. 'It's Sarah, Garrett,' she told him softly.

He gave a self-derisive laugh. 'I know exactly who you are. Do you know who I am? Let me tell you,' he added before she could even attempt to answer him. 'I'm the man who is going to make slow love to you. Until all you know and feel is me. *That's* who I am!'

Her breath came in shallow gasps. 'I want that,

Garrett, I want that so much!'

'Then let's go.' He surged out of the water with her in his arms, kicking off his shoes as he stepped out on to the side. 'Sarah and I are going to dry off.' He looked challengingly at his family and her father, water streaming off the two of them.

'We won't bother to hold dinner for you,' Jonathan answered drily.

Garrett's mouth was taut. 'You're quite welcome to go back to Washington with Father if you want to,' he bit out.

'I don't think we want to. Do we?' He looked questioningly at his wife, his eyes twinkling with humour.

Shelley smiled, her eyes teasingly bright. 'I'm enjoying myself far too much to want to leave just yet,' she told her husband lightly.

'We're staying, Garrett,' Jonathan drawled.

He nodded tersely, striding in the direction of the house.

'Do you mind?' he rasped suddenly.

'What?' Sarah blinked up at him with spiky lashes.

He gave an impatient sigh. 'That they all know we're about to make love to each other.'

It *had* been a little like making an announcement in the local newspaper, but she could see the humour of the situation, and maybe if he could too it would lighten his tension. 'Do you think *they* minded?' she drawled.

'I think they're enjoying the situation immensely!' He scowled.

She ran a finger down the dampness of his chest. 'Then why shouldn't we?' she coaxed.

The tension began to ebb from his body, and he gave a rueful smile. 'Yes, why the hell shouldn't we?' he dismissed lightly, pushing open her bedroom door to kick it shut behind them. 'Starting right now,' he murmured huskily, his lips coming down on hers.

She heatedly kissed him back, feeling herself lowered to the floor to stand in front of him, their bodies clinging together wetly.

Garrett pulled back as she gave an involuntary shiver of cold as his wet clothing touched her body. 'A hot shower for both of us first, I think.' He watched her as he began to strip off his shirt. 'I don't want you to expire from hypothermia!'

Her mouth twisted wryly as she made no effort to take off her bikini. It had been one thing for him to feel her nakedness the night before, it was quite something else to just calmly take off her only clothing in front of him in broad daylight. 'I don't think there's much chance of that with you around!'

'Nevertheless,' he touched the chill of her arms, 'you are cold.'

Her gaze flickered away from his uncertainly. 'Could I—use the bathroom first?'

He frowned, looking at her questioningly. 'Sarah, are you shy with me?'

Her lids flew wide angrily, only to relax slightly as she saw the gentleness of his expression. 'Yes,' she admitted gruffly.

'If you would rather we didn't——'

'Oh, it isn't that!' She blushed at how heated her protest had been. 'I just—I'd like to shower first.'

He watched her closely. 'Didn't you ever shower with your husband?'

'No,' she answered flatly, wishing now that she had just forgotten her shyness and stripped; it would have been better than being subjected to all these questions.

Garrett smiled. 'Then please use the bathroom first,' he invited softly. 'I'll go to my room and get some fresh clothes while I'm waiting.'

She had been relieved when he brought her to her bedroom, knowing she couldn't have shared his bed with him, the one he had shared with Amanda during their marriage.

'Garrett,' she stopped him at the door, 'why did you want to know about David just now?' she frowned.

'Because I wasn't about to let you refuse to share anything with me that you had shared with him,' he told her bluntly.

She nodded understanding before going into the adjoining bathroom, thinking how little she had really shared with David. They had had their careers in common, had felt a kind of love for each other, but it hadn't been anywhere near what she and Garrett had already shared.

As she let the heated spray warm her body she wondered about the best way to tell the man who was about to become her lover that her husband of six months never had been!

And as she wondered that she also questioned whether or not she would be able to recapture her response of last night, or if she would also leave Garrett feeling like half a man, as she had David. Garrett wouldn't force her either, she was sure of it, but he would force a full explanation from her.

By the time she had showered and pulled on her towelling robe she was feeling much like that frightened bride on her wedding night six years ago!

She forced herself to leave the bathroom, only to find Garrett waiting in the bedroom for her, also wearing only a bathrobe. She eyed him nervously as he came towards her, visibly flinching as he reached for her. She withstood his kiss with little real response on her side, seeing his puzzlement as he sensed none of the heated response in her of the night before.

'Did he hurt you?' he probed softly.

'Who?' She blinked.

'David.'

She avoided his gaze. 'No, I—er—shouldn't you be taking a shower before you catch pneumonia?' she prompted abruptly.

'I already had one, in my own bathroom,' he dismissed absently, still watching her closely. 'Sarah, I can tell that you're frightened!'

She moistened the dryness of her lips. 'I——'

'I'm not going to do anything you don't like,' he assured her gruffly. 'I'd never do anything to hurt you.'

She closed her eyes, swallowing hard. 'You will hurt me.'

'No,' he protested, shaking his head. 'What sort of man was your husband that he instilled this fear of lovemaking in you?'

She kept her eyes closed. 'He was a good man, a sweet man.' She moistened her lips again. 'He just wasn't the right man for me.'

'We all make mistakes, Sarah,' Garrett excused gently. 'We're all fallible.'

'No!' Her eyes were wide, locked with his as the truth came out haltingly. 'David was handsome, charming, everything I could have wished for in a husband—but as soon as he touched me in bed I went numb all over!'

Garrett visibly swallowed as the enormity of what she had just said struck him. 'Just now, when you said I would hurt you, you didn't mean——'

'The way all virgins are hurt.' She nodded, holding her breath without realising she did so.

He frowned. 'Your marriage was annulled?'

'No—but it should have been. I owed David saving him that humiliation too,' she said grimly.

Garrett breathed raggedly. 'I—you—I——'

'I'm not surprised you're speechless,' she snapped self-disgustedly. 'Believe me, I haven't been too happy about my behaviour either. I ruined David's life for him, was sure I was frigid!'

'We both know the latter isn't true,' Garrett said softly. 'Where is David now?'

'He works in London. But——'

'Is he married?'

She frowned. 'Yes. But——'

'Children?'

She gave an impatient sigh as Garrett kept firing questions at her. 'A new baby. But——'

'Then you obviously didn't ruin his life for him,' Garrett soothed. 'I'll admit you made it turbulent for him for a while, but he seems to have been sensible enough to put it all behind him and get on with the rest of his life. If I didn't know it *would* hurt him I would have liked to shake him by the hand and thank him!'

'For what?' she snapped incredulously.

'For letting my bride come to me untouched.'

Sarah felt herself stop breathing altogether. He couldn't have said what she had thought he had said! Could he . . .?

'Sarah, will you marry me?' he prompted eagerly. 'Will you be my wife?'

He *had* said it. But he couldn't mean it. Could he?

CHAPTER EIGHT

SARAH looked at Garrett disbelievingly. 'You want to marry me just because I'm a virgin?'

'No,' he dismissed mockingly. 'I know today's society is promiscuous, but I doubt you're the only virgin in the world. And I can't marry them all!'

'Then——'

'But I did want to marry *you* almost from the time I saw you again. Did I ever tell you how sexy you looked that night in those pyjamas——'

'Garrett!' she cut in warningly, not at all interested in how she looked in anything at the moment.

'Okay,' he held up his hands defensively, 'but you did look——'

'Garrett, *please,*' she glared. 'You just asked me to marry you, and I'd like to know why!'

'The same reason all people marry——'

'And what is that?' she interrupted impatiently.

'*Because they love each other*,' he returned just as impatiently, his expression softening as he saw the confusion on her face. 'I do love you, Sarah. I have from the moment I saw you again.'

'Because I look like Amanda——'

'You look—are, nothing like Amanda!' he dismissed irritably. 'Oh, perhaps the colouring is the same, but that's all. You're Sarah to me, Sarah of the laughing blue eyes and beautiful body.'

She frowned. 'I don't think I could ever be sure of that.'

His eyes darkened with pain. 'I can't make my marriage to Amanda disappear——'

'I wouldn't want it to,' she assured him gently. 'If it did Jason wouldn't be here either.'

His mouth firmed, his expression bleak. 'And you love him.'

'Of course.' Her brows rose.

'And you don't love me,' he rasped flatly.

'I didn't say that——' She broke off, sighing heavily. 'Garrett, I can't just forget that you were married to my sister for five years, slept with her, had a child with her. Can you?'

'I've tried to,' he grated. 'Oh God, Sarah,' he rasped at her shocked expression. 'You know damn well that my marriage to Amanda was far from successful.'

Colour heightened her cheeks. 'What makes you think it would be any different with me? I come from the same simple but happy background, have the same——'

'I didn't love Amanda!' Garrett bit out harshly, his hands clenched at his sides.

She swallowed hard. 'Never?'

'No,' he confirmed tautly.

She wasn't stupid, she knew that plenty of physical relationships were exactly that, that they survived without the involvement of the heart. But Amanda and Garrett had felt it necessary to marry when that relationship produced a child, surely they must have loved each other then, at least! If they hadn't it made a mockery of all that she believed marriage should be. She and David had had their problems, too many for them to cope with in the end, but through it all they had tried to retain the love that had begun their relationship.

'I need time to think, Garrett——'

'Why?'

'I've had one disastrous marriage——'

'And do you think I haven't?' His eyes were hard. 'I thought with you it could be different. Hell, Sarah, I've only ever asked one other woman to marry me; I haven't asked you lightly. I'm well aware of what I'm asking of you.'

And she had been encouraging him enough since her arrival here for him to be more or less certain what her answer would be! But she hadn't thought he had marriage in mind, and even loving him as she did it was impossible—wasn't it?

'I'm just not sure, Garrett ...'

He drew in a ragged breath. 'Well, maybe when you are you can let me know!'

Sarah winced as the door slammed behind him as he left. He was a proud man, who didn't let down his guard easily, and she had injured that pride, she knew that.

But what could she do? She had expected an affair, to be freed from the coldness she knew in every other man's arms but Garrett's. She loved him, yes, but marriage——! She couldn't even contemplate it, would feel haunted by Amanda all her life.

What did she do now? She couldn't possibly stay on here after refusing Garrett's proposal. And she and her father were supposed to stay here another five days. What could she do?

She looked up with a start as her father burst into the room without knocking first; the impoliteness was completely unlike him.

'What happened?' he demanded, equally without ceremony.

She could feel the heat in her cheeks. 'You saw Garrett,' she sighed.

'Saw him?' he repeated impatiently. 'The way he drove out of here no one could have missed him!'

'Garrett has gone out?' she frowned.

'I don't know that I would call it going out,' her father snapped. 'He's left the house. What happened, Sarah?' he repeated. 'One moment the two of you were acting like—like——'

'Lovers,' she supplied softly.

'Exactly,' he nodded distractedly. 'He even told his own father to leave because he can't keep a civil tongue in his head where you're concerned, and the next thing we know is he's leaving the house himself as if pursued!'

Perhaps he was, by memories. Garrett might think he could be happy with her and forget his time with Amanda, but she doubted it would ever be possible. They would both only have to look at Jason to remember.

'It didn't work out,' she avoided, her hands thrust into the pockets of her robe.

Her father looked puzzled. 'What didn't work out?' He glanced at the completely unruffled bed, evidence that they hadn't even attempted to make love. 'Sarah, the man cares for you——'

'Dad, I don't think I want to talk about this right now——'

'It seems to me that somebody ought to talk about something.' He sighed his impatience.

She frowned at his vehemence. 'What do you mean?'

He sighed again, shaking his head. 'I'm not sure, but there's something ...'

'Yes?' she prompted tautly.

He shook his head. 'Maybe I should talk to Garrett first. I'm not really sure, and until I am ...'

'What are you talking about, Dad?' she urged irritably.

Her father looked at her as if he had suddenly remembered she were there. 'It's nothing I want to mention until I'm sure, but if I am right——'

'Yes?' She was suddenly still.

He put up his hands dismissively. 'You still haven't told me why Garrett left so suddenly.'

Sarah sighed. 'I believe I said *I* didn't want to talk about that.'

Her father's expression softened. 'Darling, I know your marriage to David was a disaster——'

'You don't know the half of it, Dad.' She shook her head regretfully.

'I know that he used to pace the bedroom most nights after you both thought I was asleep, and that you used to lie awake crying!'

A blush darkened her cheeks. 'We were incompatible, Dad. Completely,' she added pointedly.

'And Garrett's walked out because you told him that?' he said incredulously.

'No,' she dismissed, looking at her father ruefully. 'I don't think you quite understand what I'm saying about David and I——'

'I understand perfectly,' he chided gently. 'And, contrary to what everyone tells us, making love doesn't come naturally between a couple at first, it has to be worked at, built upon, and very often it doesn't even get that far. You mother and I didn't bring you up with any inhibitions about your body, but society has a way of imposing those inhibitions for you.' He shook his head. 'If you don't enjoy sex with every person you meet then you're considered abnormal, and if everyone thinks you're abnormal then you *feel* that way too. Never mind that it could just be the person you're making love *with* who could be wrong for you.'

'Oh, Dad, you make what happened between David and me sound so—so normal!' She flung her arms about him as he hugged her.

'It is,' he soothed. 'Your mother and I practised for years before we got it right,' he added teasingly.

Sarah gave him a watery smile. 'Garrett just asked me to marry him,' she revealed huskily.

'And you refused him?' he frowned.

'Not exactly.'

'But enough like it for it to sound like a no to him,' her father realised ruefully. 'Because of what you just told me?'

'God, no.' She gave a self-derisive smile. 'The last thing I am with Garrett is unresponsive!'

'I noticed,' he acknowledged drily. 'On all levels. That push into the pool earlier was a nice touch!'

'I liked it,' she nodded, relaxing a little.

'Right. Now I want you to cheer up,' her father instructed briskly. 'Garrett will be back as soon as he's calmed down, and when he does get back I have no doubt he will want to talk to you.'

She gave a forlorn sigh. 'Nothing will have changed.'

'You mean to turn him down?'

'Dad, I can't marry Amanda's husband!'

He drew in a harsh breath. 'She was my daughter, and I loved her, but even from the grave she's ruining lives!'

'Dad!'

'Darling, if what I think about her is true——! She may have been unhappy, but it doesn't excuse—— I'm not going to say any more about this until I've spoken to Garrett,' he told her grimly.

He had a long wait to do that; Garrett didn't return for dinner, didn't come back to the house at all that night.

Sarah worried about him, where he was, what he was thinking. She also worried about what his family thought of her because she had been the one to drive him from the house, although Shelley and Jonathan were friendly enough, and Jason spent the evening playing chess with his grandfather as if nothing were out of the ordinary or wrong.

Sarah lay awake into the early hours of the morning listening for the sound of Garrett's car returning, and when it didn't she fell into a restless sleep that left her with a headache the next morning.

Once again the men seemed to have gone off on their own pursuits; the maid informed her that they had gone to play golf. As her father had never played the game she could only assume Jason and Jonathan were going to teach it to him.

'You really shouldn't worry about Garrett,' Shelly cajoled her as soon as the pale-faced Sarah joined her on the patio for breakfast, the other woman putting down the book she had been reading. 'He's a grown man, and if he chooses to go off like a sulky child——'

'I hurt him,' she defended.

'I'm sure he had good reason to go off the way that he did,' Shelley acknowledged lightly. 'But he always was too volatile. Fond of him as I am, I'm glad I realised before it was too late that Jonathan would suit me much better as a husband.'

Sarah sipped her coffee, clearing some of the cobwebs that seemed to have formed in her brain. 'What do you mean?'

The other woman gave a rueful smile. 'I knew

Garrett before I knew Jonathan; we thought we were in love, but we were both very young, and—well, I met Jonathan and realised what real love was,' she shrugged.

'Garrett must have been very upset at losing you to his brother,' Sarah said faintly; she had had no idea Garrett had once loved this woman. Although she remembered Jonathan's comment now the first day she had arrived here, a totally unrelated comment it had seemed to her, about Shelley and Garrett being 'just friends'. At the time she had wondered whether Shelley would be annoyed to see her husband disappear with *her*, had been a little surprised when he took her to mean *he* might be jealous of Garrett with his wife. Now she understood the remark, also the rapport that seemed to exist between Shelley and Garrett.

Shelley grimaced. 'That was the first time I had seen Garrett's temper in action! It's happened a lot more over the years, but that first time was definitely the worst!'

'You must have been very young,' she frowned.

'Both nineteen,' the other woman nodded. 'And Jonathan was twenty-four. After months of dating Garrett it was love at first sight for Jonathan and me. Garrett was furious,' she recalled indulgently.

'He still cares for you very much——'

'Hey!' Shelley chided. 'I only told you this to try and cheer you up; don't start imagining love where it doesn't exist,' she said reprovingly. 'Of course he cares for me; I feel the same way about him. But it isn't that sort of love. I only told you

about the two of us to try and show you that when
his emotions are involved he's even less tolerant
than usual. But he'll come around, you'll see.'

'You make him sound like a tyrant!' said Sarah
ruefully.

'He is,' the other woman confirmed lightly.
'He's used to total control on a film set, to moving
characters to his will, and he forgets he can't do
the same thing with real people. Last night you
thwarted his will.'

Sarah gave a reluctant smile. 'Are you sure you
married the right brother? You seem to know
Garrett so well!'

Shelley laughed softly. 'Believe me, Jonathan is
much more sweet-tempered.'

Sarah sighed. 'It was my fault Garrett left the
way he did——'

'Now don't start blaming yourself again,'
Shelley rebuked. 'He's the one who's gone off in a
sulk.'

'Yes, but——'

'I won't have you blaming yourself,' the other
woman said firmly. 'And if you aren't going to eat
any breakfast I suggest we go for a drive and find
somewhere to have an early lunch.'

Sarah looked uncertain.

'You aren't going to sit here and wait for him,'
she was told determinedly. 'Let him think you
don't give a damn.'

'But I——'

'Love him,' Shelley finished briskly. 'Yes, I
know. We all know how you feel, including

Garrett. But after worrying you all night——' She gave Sarah a searching look. 'Giving you a *sleepless* night,' she amended. 'It will do him good to get home and have to wait for *you* to get back!'

Sarah followed the other woman out to the car. 'Does "sweet-tempered" Jonathan know how bossy you are?' she derided as she folded the wheelchair and put it in the back, while Shelley got behind the wheel.

Shelley grinned. 'Of course not.'

Sarah relaxed completely on the drive, very impressed when Shelley chose the permanently berthed *Queen Mary* as the 'somewhere' they stopped for lunch. Berthed at Long Beach, it was still as elegantly beautiful as it must have been during the time it sailed the Atlantic full of passengers. Now it was a hotel with several restaurants, and Sarah enjoyed the experience of being on board enormously, and she enjoyed Shelley's company even more. Whatever reserve the other woman had initially felt towards her was completely gone now.

'Hm.' Shelley looked at her watch once they were back in the car. 'Do you think we've been out long enough?'

Considering it was after three o'clock now, Sarah thought they had been out too long, and was longing to get back to the house to see if Garrett had returned yet. But she didn't like to push the other woman. 'I—er——'

Shelley laughed softly. 'Stop trying to be polite, Sarah, and tell me to drive back to the house.'

'Shelley, drive back to the house,' she dutifully instructed in her sternest voice.

The other woman chuckled, turning the car in the direction of Malibu. 'I bet you make a formidable schoolteacher!'

'Not half as formidable as the politician's wife you make!'

'Now don't forget,' Shelley warned as they neared the house. 'He's the one that walked out on you.'

The first thing Sarah saw as they turned in the driveway was Garrett's car, a red Mercedes he drove with panache. Her heart seemed to beat louder than ever, her palms were suddenly damp.

'I'm going to my room to freshen up,' Shelley excused herself as soon as they were in the house.

Sarah was glad of the time alone to search for Garrett. It didn't take long to find him, in the pool, moving through the water with long, powerful strokes of his arms, his movements mechanical, going from one end to the other with lightning speed. She didn't know whether the rest of the family's absence was through choice or forced, but from the look of him she didn't think Garrett's temper had cooled at all.

She asked for a drink and sat under an umbrella to wait for him to either tire or become bored; probably the latter from the look of him.

It was almost half an hour later when he walked out of the water and up the steps, pausing only briefly in towelling his hair as he saw her sipping her cool drink. After a narrow-eyed glare he continued towelling.

'Enjoy your swim?' she enquired lightly.

'Not particularly,' he rasped, the towel draped about his neck now.

She sighed softly at his unyielding attitude. 'If you would rather not talk——'

'Talk!' he grated harshly. 'What the hell good has talking done me so far?' His eyes glittered angrily.

She bit her bottom lip painfully. 'I'm sorry if I've hurt you——'

'Don't flatter yourself,' he scorned. 'I'm angry, not hurt, angry at your narrow-mindedness.'

Sarah shook her head. 'I can't——'

'Marry me. I know,' he dismissed harshly. 'How about an affair, could you live with that?'

She paled at the contempt in his voice. 'You aren't even trying to understand——'

'Oh, but I understand perfectly.' Garrett's eyes were narrowed to emerald slits. 'I'm good enough to have an affair with but not to have around permanently as a husband!'

I thought an affair was all you wanted——'

'And now you know that it isn't you're running scared——'

'I'm still here,' she reminded him tautly.

'Where the hell have you been all morning?' he burst out furiously.

She stood up abruptly. 'Where were you all night?' she returned just as angrily.

His mouth twisted. 'I suppose if I told you I'd picked up a woman in a bar and gone home with her for the night you would believe me!'

She gave an audible gasp, breathing deeply to calm her anger. 'I would believe you just as easily if you told me you spent the night alone,' she finally bit out in a controlled voice.

He looked at her coldly. 'I spent the night sitting in my car staring at the ocean.'

'Oh, Garrett——'

He held up a silencing hand. 'I tried to find some way out of this tangle, but you're right, there isn't one, not without hurting a lot of innocent people.' He sighed. 'So we'll part at the end of this holiday and never see each other again.'

Never? She couldn't bear that. 'But when we see Jason again——'

'I'll make sure I'm not around,' he bit out grimly.

'Garrett——'

He avoided the hand she put out towards him. 'It's for the best, Sarah.' His eyes were bleak.

Maybe it was, but she couldn't bear the thought of not seeing him again. 'I love you, Garrett,' she choked emotionally.

Pleasure flared in his eyes, only to be quickly dampened, leaving him looking more defeated than ever. 'I love you, too,' he sighed. 'But this seems to be one of those times when loving each other isn't enough.'

She gave a choked sob, turning to run into the house, her tears blinding her as she ran into the solid wall of a male chest. 'I'm sorry——'

'It's all ri— my God, Sarah, what's wrong?'

Jonathan demanded concernedly.

She kept her face averted. 'I'm sorry, I—I have to go to my room!' She moved out of his arms, brushing the tears away, desperately seeking the sanctuary of her bedroom, realising her mistake as soon as she was alone.

Garrett had a right to be angry with her; what was she *doing* turning down the love of the man she cared for more than anything else on this earth? Of course she had loved her sister, and it was a tragedy that their marriage hadn't worked out, but her father was right; she and Garrett deserved their chance at happiness together. If it didn't work out at least they would have *tried*!

She hurried back to the pool, hoping he was still there.

'When I want your opinion I'll ask for it,' Garrett was telling Jonathan, his voice raised. 'Just don't try to tell me how to run my life, not when you've made such a mess of your own!'

Sarah came to an abrupt halt in the doorway out on to the patio, loath to interrupt the two men when they were glaring at each other so grimly. Obviously Jonathan had come to her defence, and received a tongue-lashing for his effort.

'I made one mistake, Garrett——'

'It wasn't a mistake, you knew exactly what you were doing,' accused Garrett viciously.

Jonathan was very pale. 'I couldn't help myself——'

'I don't want to hear your excuses, Jonathan,' Garrett derided harshly. 'I just want you to stay away from Sarah. If you go near her again I'll kill you.'

'I've told you I won't,' his brother sighed, 'I just—she's so much like Amanda!'

'She's nothing like Amanda,' Garrett denied harshly. 'Even Amanda wasn't like the Amanda *you* thought she was!'

'She was so beautiful, so——'

'Even now you can't forget what you had with her, can you?' Garrett scorned. 'You have Shelley, your career, and you still think of the woman who briefly shared your bed!'

Sarah didn't want to hear any more; she had heard more than enough, and she fell back out of sight, leaning weakly against the wall.

Amanda and *Jonathan*?

CHAPTER NINE

SARAH stared sightlessly at the wall. Amanda and *Jonathan*. She still couldn't believe it—no, that wasn't quite true, she *could* believe it, it was just so hard to take in.

She believed it because of Garrett's anger towards Amanda, Jonathan's pleasure that she looked so much like her sister, William Kingham's resentment for the same reason, Shelley's dislike of Amanda, and most of all, because of her own father's description of Amanda being wilful and selfish. Amanda would have to be both those things to have had an affair with a man whose wife couldn't fight back on equal grounds.

What she couldn't understand, when the family obviously knew of the affair, was why it hadn't split the whole family apart. Unless, perhaps, Amanda had died before that could happen? Amanda had seemed so sure about the divorce when she came home, and Garrett had seemed equally sure that there wouldn't be one. Maybe he hadn't realised just how deeply Amanda's feelings for his brother went.

How could Amanda and Jonathan have done that to Shelley, to Garrett?

Here was the 'something' that had been bothering her father, she was sure of it. What would it do to him to learn what his elder daughter had done to her own husband and sister-in-law?

It was evidence of how far her feelings for Garrett had come that she didn't instantly blame him for Amanda's infidelity, accuse him of forcing her into another man's arms! No matter how unhappy her sister had been she should never have entered into an affair with Jonathan! It had been unforgivably cruel to Shelley, and disloyal to Garrett.

How he must have hated Amanda for what she had done to him and Shelley.

And *she* had rejected him as if he were used goods!

Amanda had been a fool to reject a man like Garrett, but Sarah was even more determined now not to be as foolish. Her sister hadn't wanted her husband, that was obvious, but *she* did, and if he would still have her, she would marry him and try to make him happy for the rest of his life.

He didn't put in an appearance for dinner that night either.

Sarah had dressed with care; the silky blue dress that clung alluringly to her curves was the same blue as her eyes, her hair was newly washed, gleaming with vitality, her make-up perfect.

And Garrett wasn't there as they sat down to dinner, didn't put in an appearance during the meal either.

When she had gone back to her room earlier he and Jonathan had still been arguing, and she had decided not to intrude. Now she wished she had.

'Garrett's sulking again,' said Shelley ruefully when they were all having coffee.

Sarah glanced at Jonathan. He had been very subdued during dinner; obviously the argument between him and Garrett had gone on for some time after she had retreated so hurriedly, not wanting them to realise she had overheard their conversation, not wanting Garrett to realise she knew of the humiliation he had suffered at Amanda's hands.

There could be no doubt in anyone's mind that Jonathan loved his wife, just as she didn't doubt, from his conversation with Garrett, that in his own way he had loved Amanda too, still thought of her often. How he could care for two women at the same time, even though one of those women was now dead, was beyond her. From Shelley's attitude to Amanda it seemed obvious she had known of her husband's affair, but whatever friction it had caused at the time Shelley had now put it all behind her.

Poor Garrett: the two women he had cared for in his life before her had both preferred Jonathan. If he would accept her love after all that had been said he need never doubt her, she wanted only him, always.

'Dad isn't sulking,' Jason defended. 'He had some work to do.'

'Jason, we all know he's locked himself away in the study because he's still angry with Sarah,' Shelley chided gently.

Sarah's eyes widened. In the study? 'He's here in the house?'

'Mm,' the other woman nodded. 'And the door isn't literally locked,' she encouraged.

Sarah stood up slowly. Would Garret listen to her when she told him she realised she had made a mistake, or would he remain angry with her? Whatever his reaction, she had to speak to him.

'Thanks.' She squeezed Shelley's arm gratefully.

'Watch out for flying glasses. Or bottles,' the other woman warned lightly. 'The last I heard he had ordered a bottle of Scotch to be taken in to him!'

Sarah couldn't imagine Garrett drunk; he thought it beneath his arrogant dignity to be anything less than completely in control of his actions, and she hated the idea of being responsible for his depression.

She needn't have worried about seeing him drunk; the bottle of Scotch stood untouched on the desk, with Garrett sitting behind the desk staring at it morosely.

'Can I come in?' she queried lightly.

He focused on her with narrowed eyes, looking very tired. 'What do you want?'

Sarah moistened her lips, closing the door quietly behind her, wondering what he would do if she were to say 'you'! For she did want him, couldn't imagine life without him now, had been a fool ever to deny either of them, whether her loyalty to Amanda was warranted or not. Even if he and Amanda had been happy together they still deserved their own chance of happiness.

She stepped forward, taking a deep breath. 'You,' she told him huskily.

He leant back slowly in his chair, the brown shirt and trousers tailored to his body. 'What?' he rasped irritably.

She swallowed hard. 'I made a mistake, Garrett——'

'When?'

She drew in a ragged breath. 'When I told you I couldn't marry you.'

'Why?'

She swallowed hard; he certainly wasn't about to make this easy for her. But then why should he? It shouldn't have mattered who he had been married to in the past, it was whom he loved now that mattered.

'Because I love you,' she told him huskily.

His eyes were narrowed. 'You loved me yesterday, and this afternoon too, if you're to be believed, but you still turned me down. I wonder what happened to change your mind?' he mused bitterly.

'I——'

'Tell me,' he cut in silkily. 'Did you get your purse back earlier? I noticed it at the pool after you left this afternoon.'

Sarah hadn't even realised she had left it behind until one of the maids had returned it with her tea, but it was obvious Garrett suspected she might have gone in search of it and overheard his

conversation with Jonathan. If she admitted she
had, would that damn her in his eyes, when in
reality it had been the desolation of facing the rest
of her life without him that had changed her mind
about marrying him? It didn't even sound
believeable to her. And yet it was the *truth*.

She sighed. 'You're right, Garrett, I did
overhear you and Jonathan.'

'And?'

She looked at him sharply. 'I know now that
Amanda had an affair with Jonathan while she was
married to you.'

He drew in a sharp breath. 'And?' he prompted
again.

She shook her head. 'I only listened for a few
minutes, but it—it was enough.'

'I see,' he bit out grimly, his eyes cold. 'And
now you've decided you want me.'

'I've always wanted you,' she choked. 'I was
coming to tell you——'

'That now that you know your sainted sister
had an affair you feel it's okay to marry me!' He
was furiously angry, his eyes accusing.

'No——'

'Yes,' he insisted contemptuously. 'Thanks—
but no, thanks. I married one woman for all the
wrong reasons; I'm not about to repeat the
mistake. I invited you here because I hoped you
would see for yourself, realise——' He shook his
head. 'You're too blinded by the past to see the
sort of future we could have had together.'

'But I'm not! I came to tell you——'

'Don't you understand, Sarah?' He stood up forcefully. 'I don't want you any more!'

She paled at his cruelty. 'If that's true your emotions are very fickle——'

'Not half as fickle as yours',' he accused disgustedly. 'Did you really think you could overhear me discussing Amanda's affair with Jonathan, come here and apologise and everything would be all right?'

'That isn't the way it happened,' she insisted heatedly. 'As soon as I left you earlier I realised I had made a mistake, that I couldn't live the rest of my life without you, I didn't come in search of my bag earlier, I came back to tell you I realised I had made a mistake!'

He looked at her coldly. 'Even if that were the truth——'

'It is!'

'But *I* could never be sure of that, could I?' He shook his head.

Too late, she had left it too late to realise that he could have had a dozen wives before her, all of them related to her, and it wouldn't have mattered as long as it was *her* he loved now!

'Garrett, I love you,' she choked. 'If you no longer want to marry me, at least—at least take me as a lover!' She looked at him pleadingly.

'No,' he refused bluntly.

'Garrett, please——'

'I said no, damn it!' he bit out viciously. 'I acquired one wife through trickery; I'm not about to get another one the same way!'

She flinched as if he had physically struck her.
'You think I would—that I——'

'Why not?' he scorned. 'A Harvey woman
doesn't like to be thwarted when she "wants"
something!'

'You——' She was trembling so badly she could
barely stand. 'Garrett——'

'I'm leaving here early tomorrow,' he cut in
coldly. 'I have to go to Spain for a few days. Stay
and enjoy the rest of your holiday; I shouldn't be
back until you're safely back in England.'

Sarah barely felt him brush by her on his way
out of the room, too numb to feel anything at that
moment.

And when she did feel again the pain was almost
too much to bear; dry sobs racked her body, and
she was sure that the pain was never going to stop.

True to his word, Garrett had left the house by the
time Sarah put in an appearance at nine o'clock
the next morning.

Unlike the other mornings when she had joined
Shelley for breakfast the other men were still
sitting on the patio with her, and they all looked as
depressed as Sarah felt.

After the harsh words that had passed between
herself and Garrett she hadn't felt able to sleep,
had lain awake on her bed most of the night, heard
someone, she had presumed Garrett, leave the
house just after dawn; the car certainly hadn't
returned. She had listened for its return until her
head ached and it was late enough for her to get up

and stop feigning sleep.

Coming out of her room some time later had been the worst thing she had to face, but as she knew the maid must be waiting for her to leave so that she could clean it, and she could hardly hide in there all day, she had finally forced herself to face the others.

Although they must be aware of the fact that Garrett had left the house, they all greeted her warmly enough, her father's gaze lingering concernedly on the paleness of her cheeks she had tried to disguise with blusher. She gave him a bright smile, knowing it would do little to hide the fact that she looked ill, her eyes sunken and bruised-looking.

She looked anxiously towards Jason, sure he must blame her for his father's abrupt departure; the sympathy she read in his eyes was almost her undoing.

'Coffee?' Shelley neatly smoothed the moment of awkwardness.

'Thank you,' she accepted woodenly, taking the cup, her hands shaking slightly.

'Dad's gone,' Jason told her softly.

'Yes,' she acknowledged tautly.

'He left early this morning,' Jason continued.

'Yes.' Her reply was sharper this time.

'Do you——'

'Jason, could we not talk about your father?' she requested stiffly.

He looked at her challengingly. 'I only wanted to know if he told you where he was going.'

'I'm sorry.' She blushed at her thoughtlessness. 'I thought he would have told you ... He said something about needing to go to Spain for a while.'

'Spain?' Jason repeated frowningly. 'Why on earth would he go there?'

'I have no idea,' she dismissed brittlely. 'Something to do with the film he's making, I imagine.'

'But——'

'Jason, leave her alone,' interrupted Jonathan sharply. 'Can't you see Sarah is upset?'

Jason flashed him a resentful glare. 'Of course I can see she's upset——'

'Then don't keep asking her senseless questions!' his uncle rasped.

'It's all right, Jonathan,' Sarah soothed the suddenly tense atmosphere. 'Jason is just concerned——'

'That doesn't excuse——'

'Doesn't excuse what?' Jason challenged his uncle. 'Why don't you just mind your own business—and take your hands off her!' he warned furiously, his gaze fixed on Jonathan's hand as it rested comfortingly on Sarah's.

'Jason!' she gasped, never having heard him use that vicious tone with anyone before.

He stood up angrily, his body tense. 'He has no right to——'

'Why don't we all just calm down?' Shelley suggested soothingly. 'Jason sit down and finish your breakfast.'

'I don't want it,' he refused defiantly.

'Don't speak to your aunt like that,' warned Jonathan harshly.

Green eyes glittered angrily at green. 'Or what?' Jason challenged scornfully. 'You'll hit me? You aren't man enough——'

'Jason, that will be enough,' his grandfather ordered with quiet authority.

Jason looked abashed by the rebuke, although his expression remained rebellious. 'You don't understand, Grandad——'

'Oh, I think I do,' he cut in gently. 'I understand perfectly,' he added pointedly.

Sarah didn't understand this flare of tempers at all. They were all a little tense after Garrett's departure, yes, but this . . .! Jason actually seemed to hate his uncle at this moment.

He looked uncertainly at his grandfather. 'You do?' he quavered.

'Yes.' Sarah's father nodded slowly.

'But—how?'

'I guessed,' his grandfather told him softly. 'It hasn't been too difficult the last few days. You?'

'The same,' Jason grated. 'Weeks ago!'

'Would you like to go somewhere quiet and we can talk about it?' his grandfather encouraged gently.

'Yes, I think I would,' he rasped, looking resentfully at the stunned faces about him.

Sarah's father squeezed her shoulder as he moved to join Jason in the house. 'I'm sure Jonathan will explain it all to you.' His gaze challenged the other man. 'Jason needs me more at this moment,' he added, regretfully following Jason inside.

Sarah watched them go, a puzzled frown marring her brow, and she became even more confused as she turned to see how pale Shelley and Jonathan had become. 'I don't understand any of this.' She shook her head.

'I do,' said Jonathan dully.

'So do I,' Shelley told her flatly, although it was to Jonathan she looked as she said it.

He raised his head slowly to meet his wife's gaze, his eyes dark with pain. 'You do?' he prompted weakly.

Shelley drew in a deep controlling breath. 'Yes.'

'But——'

'Darling, poor Sarah is still completely in the dark about what everyone's been talking about,' she reminded him gently.

'I know,' he dismissed. 'But how long have you—— When did you——'

'A long time ago,' Shelley sighed. 'Now don't you think it's time Sarah was told what this is all about?' she prompted huskily.

Jonathan swallowed hard. 'I don't understand—why did you never——'

'We can talk in a moment, darling,' his wife soothed, turning to Sarah. 'What Jason somehow seems to have found out, and your father seems to have guessed since coming here, is that——'

'Garrett isn't Jason's father—*I* am,' Jonathan cut in flatly.

'Why the hell did you tell either of them that?' rasped a coldly angry voice.

They all turned to look at Garrett as he strode furiously towards them.

CHAPTER TEN

'IT's a lie, Shelley,' Garrett rasped, his eyes narrowed. 'Don't listen to a word he——'

'Garrett,' she interrupted softly, 'I've known the truth for some time.'

A nerve pulsed in his cheek. 'How?'

'Amanda took great delight in telling me just before she left you that last time,' she revealed sadly.

'Amanda!' Garrett grated accusingly, his eyes cold as he looked at Sarah.

She flinched under that silent onslaught, knew that in that moment he hated everyone and everything that reminded him of the woman who had been his wife, the mother of his brother's child.

She was still reeling under the shock of knowing that Jonathan was Jason's father, was having difficulty taking in the full significance of Amanda being pregnant with Jonathan's child *before* she married Garrett. What she did know for certain was that her father had realised during his visit here what she was too blind to see, that *this* was the 'something' he had guessed at, not just Amanda's affair.

But it still remained that Jonathan and Amanda had had an affair *before* she married Garrett——!

'Sarah,' Shelley softly probed her shock, 'I don't want to hurt you, I'm sure none of us want to do that; we know that you loved your sister very much———'

'I want to hear the truth,' she cut in firmly. 'No matter what it is.'

Shelley nodded understandingly. 'Then I think———'

'Shelley, no,' Garrett cut in harshly. 'I'm sorry you ever had to know the truth, but telling Sarah will only succeed in hurting *her*.'

Sarah looked up at him, hope flaring within her at his attempt to shield her. Maybe he had changed his mind ...! 'Garrett, before I hear the truth I want you to know that I meant what I said yesterday, and that it had nothing to do with overhearing you and Jonathan talking.'

'Why the hell do you think I came back if it wasn't because I realised you've never told me anything but the truth?' he rasped. 'Even if it has been painful on occasion,' he added ruefully.

Her love for him brightened her eyes. 'After we've finished talking here ...?'

'*We'll* talk,' he nodded. 'But this isn't going to be pleasant. For any of us.' He looked at the other couple.

'Garrett, Jason knows too,' Sarah told him softly.

Anger flashed in the turbulent green eyes. 'Who the hell———'

'No one,' Shelley sighed heavily. 'He just seems to have worked it out for himself.'

'Damn!' Garrett grated viciously. 'I wondered why he refused to come to you and Jonathan this time when I had to go away, why he pulled that disappearing act and went to see Geoffrey and Sarah! I have to go to him——'

'Dad's with him,' Sarah soothed. 'I think it would be best if you left them alone for a while. Take heart from the fact that he's known for some time, Garrett, and it hasn't changed his feelings towards you.'

'Oh, God.' He sat down weakly, closing his eyes. 'I hope he realised that I *am* his father, that I have been since he was placed in my arms seconds after he was born.'

Sarah clasped his hand, willing her strength into him. 'I'm sure he does.'

He looked at her gratefully, both of them knowing the time for their own explanations would come later, that Jason came first with both of them at this moment.

She looked enquiringly at the pale-faced Jonathan, the shock of Jason's real parentage receding now as she waited for his explanation. He looked uncertainly at Shelley, the pain of self-recrimination in his eyes.

'It's all right,' she assured him huskily. 'I know most of it anyway.'

He flushed. 'How could Amanda——'

'Don't be a fool, Jonathan,' Garrett scorned. 'When Amanda was thwarted she could do anything!'

'But why should she want to hurt Shelley?' His

brother shook his head dazedly.

'Because she got in the way of what Amanda wanted,' Garrett said grimly. 'You had made it obvious you didn't want to marry her, and when you became a senator her bitterness became too much for her, and she told Shelley of your affair. God, she proposed to *me* because she knew you didn't want her!'

Sarah looked at Garrett as if she had never seen him before; *Amanda* had proposed to him! Then the other woman *he* had proposed to hadn't been Amanda at all, it had to have been Shelley, and he had agreed to marry Amanda to protect Shelley. Did he still love Shelley? Not in that way, she was sure of it.

Jonathan looked as if Garrett had dealt him a physical blow. 'But I thought—I always thought——'

'What? That I loved her, that I wanted to marry her?' Garrett derided hardly. 'I never did. She was shallow and selfish. But she carried a Kingham child. And she threatened to destroy that child unless I made her my wife!'

'No!' Sarah and Jonathan cried together.

'Yes,' he bit out. 'She also had several other conditions attached to the marriage, but when I wasn't agreeable to those she settled for what she could get: my ring on her finger.'

'Wh-what other conditions?' Jonathan frowned.

A ruddy hue darkened Garrett's rigidly clenched cheeks. 'None of your damned business!

I married her, I gave *your* child a name—but as soon as he was born he became *my* child!'

'I was a fool.' Jonathan buried his face in his hands. 'I met Amanda at one of your parties, was dazzled by her, wanted her,' he added weakly. 'I tried not to, but—oh God, Shelley, it had nothing to do with not loving you!' He looked pleadingly at his wife.

'I knew that,' she clasped his hand, 'I've always known that. Otherwise I would have left you years ago.'

'Amanda was the only other woman——'

'I know that too,' Shelley said sadly. 'At first I thought it was because I'm in this chair——'

'No!' denied Jonathan harshly. 'It was never that.' He shook his head vehemently. 'She was just totally unlike anyone else I had ever met. I was dazzled,' he said again. 'And then it was all over; she was pregnant with my child but said she was marrying Garrett.'

'She wanted to be at the centre of the stage, Jonathan,' his brother scorned. 'If not as the wife of a politician then as the wife of a film director. Unfortunately for her, that was as far as I'd let her go. She wasn't pleased at having her acting career ended before it had begun. But being the wife of a rich man, and *acting* the part, was better than nothing at all!'

'She told me she was marrying you because she loved you,' Jonathan groaned.

Garrett gave him a pitying look. 'To hurt you, only to hurt you. We despised each other at best.'

Jonathan drew in a shuddering breath. 'I've ruined so many lives——'

'Not mine,' Garrett dismissed, looking at Sarah. 'Almost, but not quite,' he murmured intensely.

'Jason hates me——'

'He's angry,' Garrett corrected as he turned back to his brother. 'And he has every right to be,' he added grimly. 'When he feels like talking to us we'll both go and see him, try to explain. But remember that he's *my* son, Jonathan. Your blood tie may be stronger than mine, but——'

'God, I'd never even try to come between the two of you,' gasped Jonathan. 'He tolerates me, he *loves* you.'

'Our marriage has survived too, Jonathan,' Shelley assured him softly.

'Talking of marriages,' Garrett cut in briskly. 'You'll excuse us if Sarah and I go off and discuss ours—in private?'

The other couple were talking in soft murmurs as Sarah and Garrett left the room, and she had a feeling they were going to be fine.

They went to Garrett's bedroom, standing awkwardly apart from each other.

Garrett suddenly gave a shuddering sigh, grasping her arms. 'Would you mind if we— postponed our talk for now, important as it is, and I just belatedly took you up on your offer of yesterday?'

She gazed up at him with all the tenderness inside her. 'I wish you would,' she invited.

'Oh, Sarah!' He crushed her to him. 'Sarah, I love you!'

She rained kisses over his face and chest. 'I love you too. I love you! I'm so sorry for what my sister——'

'Hush.' He put gentle fingertips over her trembling lips. 'At this moment, this beautiful moment of your giving yourself to me, we're only going to think of each other.'

They undressed each other as if in a dream, moving together with searching caresses, Garrett showing her all the heady delight she knew she was capable of in his arms.

When his body merged with hers she knew only the briefest of discomfort, closing silkily about him as they moved together in building harmony, their cries merged as they reached the summit of desire.

They lay in each other's arms, Sarah slowly caressing Garrett in the aftermath of their passion, loving the male beauty of him, his body all gold and bronze planes. And he was completely hers, she was sure of it.

'I was wrong,' he groaned huskily. 'I didn't die; I feel more alive than I ever have before!'

'I was always glad before that you never brought me here, but now I know I had nothing to fear; you never made love to Amanda here or anywhere else, did you,' she said huskily.

Garrett stiffened. 'What makes you say that?' He looked down at her guardedly.

She smiled, moving to look down at him,

smoothing the frown from his brow. 'The fact that the first night you came to the cottage you fell asleep in the chair and woke up pushing me away believing it was Amanda, because you always insisted on staying at a hotel when you visited us so that my parents would never know the two of you had separate bedrooms—and the fact that sharing a bed with Amanda was one of those conditions you *weren't* agreeable to!'

His mouth twisted. 'You worked all that out, did you?' he drawled.

She looked at him steadily. 'Yes—finally.'

He sighed, moving up the bed to sit back against the pillows, his arms possessive about her. 'I didn't want her,' he sighed.

'But she wanted you.'

'Sarah, she wasn't really all bad, she was unhappy because Jonathan really loved Shelley, and——'

'That last time she left you, she told us she was going to divorce you; would you have done *anything* she asked to prevent that?'

'I don't know,' he groaned. 'I knew her conditions before she walked out, and I—I suppose I would eventually have accepted them.' His face was pale. 'It wasn't enough for her that she had everything money could buy, that she had the admiration of all her friends, a child who adored her; she was always leaving me and blackmailing me with the threat of divorce to get what she wanted, and that last time——'

'She wanted you,' Sarah realised weakly.

'She wanted a normal marriage, yes,' he bit out.

'I can understand that.'

'Sarah!'

'Let me tell you something, Garrett, something I think you have a right to know——'

His arms tightened about her. 'I'm not letting you go,' he ground out. 'No matter what family secret you're about to tell me.'

She gave a gentle smile of understanding; they had come through so much, nothing would part them now. 'I'm not letting *you* go.'

'Then what——'

'There were once two sisters,' she began. 'The elder, more beautiful one——'

'I think I'm a better judge of that than you are, and you——'

'—and the young, shy one,' she continued with a censorious look. 'The elder sister went off to Hollywood, hoping to one day see her name up in lights, but instead she came back with a prince——' She gave Garrett a reproving frown as he snorted. 'A beautiful Golden Prince who dazzled and mesmerised the younger sister, so much so that any man she met after him came a very poor second——'

'Sarah . . .?'

'The elder sister lived with her Golden Prince in the Golden Land, while the younger sister pined for him in a land that had suddenly lost all its sunshine——'

'Sweetheart, you don't have to tell me all this!' he groaned, his arms tight.

'Now the beautiful sister wasn't happy with her Golden Prince, and finally she left him, and when she told the younger sister that she intended to divorce her Golden Prince, she was glad, hoped that he would finally see her, fall in love with *her*. Before I saw you again, Garrett,' Sarah's voice had changed from the story-telling lilt, trembling emotionally, 'Amanda was dead. And I felt as if I had helped kill her because I wanted you myself! I hated you, but I hated myself more!' She buried her face against his chest. 'I attacked you that day because of my guilt, I convinced myself I hated you for making me care about you.'

'And when the "Golden Prince" did see you, fell in love with you, you refused me for the same reason!' he groaned.

'Yes,' she whispered huskily. 'I married David hoping to give my father the grandchildren he had always wanted, and instead I found I couldn't respond to him. Two minutes after seeing you again I knew the reason why: my love for you had never died.'

Garrett swallowed convulsively. 'Sarah . . .! Is it all going to be over now? Are you going to marry me so that *we* can be the ones to give your father more grandchildren?'

She nodded. 'Amanda was very unhappy as your wife, but it was the life she chose for herself; I *know* we'll be happy together.'

'So do I!' he said fervently. 'I've waited long enough for you.'

'Your father, Garrett,' she said after a long

silence. 'Do you think he'll ever accept me as your wife?'

'Maybe. Maybe not.' He shrugged. 'I never told him that Jason wasn't my son, and he always believed Amanda had tricked me into marriage; they didn't get on. But it will be his loss if he doesn't accept you.'

'Jonathan and Shelley will be all right, won't they?' she frowned.

'Jonathan was a damned fool over Amanda, and he almost did the same thing over you——'

'Me?' She looked startled.

'It wasn't me who came into your bedroom your first day here,' Garrett told her regretfully. 'I could have killed Jonathan when you accused me of invading your privacy by sneaking into your room to touch you while you were sleeping! I knew it had to be him. You were like a ghost to him, but as he got to know you he realised you weren't really like Amanda at all. It's as well that he did.' His eyes were cold. 'I would have torn him apart if he had tried to touch you again!'

Sarah hated the thought of Jonathan being driven to come to her room, of his touching her, but she pitied him too. 'He was in love with a person who never existed.' She shook her head sadly.

Garrett nodded grimly. 'Except in his imagination!'

'Poor Shelley,' she sighed. 'I'm not sure I could have remained silent all these years.'

'She deserves better,' he agreed. 'But it's

Jonathan she loves.'

'She was one of the things you once spoke of "giving up", wasn't she?' Sarah prompted softly.

'I thought she was,' he acknowledged slowly. 'Although in retrospect I think I just didn't like losing her to Jonathan. The accident while they were still on their honeymoon didn't help——'

'I had no idea . . .!' Sarah gasped. 'How awful for them both!'

Garrett nodded. 'I told myself that if I had never introduced them she would never have fallen in love with him, never have married him, and wouldn't have been in that particular place at that time. I was still feeling betrayed by them when Amanda came to me and suggested I be a father to her child. It seemed like suitable restitution at the time; I got Amanda and Jonathan's baby, while he had the woman I loved.' He shook his head. 'I was very young and very stupid.'

'And my sister made your life a misery,' Sarah realised.

'Not a complete misery.' He grinned down at her. 'She also gave me you!'

'But——'

'It all happened a very long time ago, Sarah,' he sighed. 'And I, for one, want to forget all about it.'

'Do you still love Shelley?' she voiced the last uncertainty she had.

'I never loved her in the way I now love you,' he answered without hesitation. 'I love her as a sister, but my pride was hurt when she chose Jonathan over me.' He smiled mischievously down at Sarah. 'Of course, if you would like to demonstrate again how much *you* love me I won't fight you.' He lay back in complete surrender.

'So I can see,' she drawled.

'Well?'

'Well, what?' she feigned innocence.

He frowned. 'Surely I wasn't that bad a tutor?' he grumbled.

'You were an excellent seducer of young women,' she assured him lightly.

'Ah.'

'Yes?' she prompted, her brows raised.

'I forgot something, didn't I?' he grinned, looking more boyish than she had ever seen him.

'I think it's a little late to worry about *that*!' Sarah derided.

'What? Oh. No, I didn't mean that,' he dismissed, moving so that she lay beneath him now. 'Although that would be rather nice.' He caressed the smooth silkiness of her flat stomach.

'You wouldn't mind having a baby so soon?' It banished that last remaining shadow that had lingered in her mind.

'No. Although I think I ought to reassure the child I *do* have how wanted he is before we give him any brothers or sisters,' Garrett added with a frown.

Sarah touched his cheek with gentle concern. 'I think you'll find he's old enough to accept and understand what happened between Amanda and Jonathan. Although I don't know if it would be fair to him to burden him with how unhappy *you* were with his mother,' she said uncertainly. 'He loves her memory so much.'

Garrett nodded. 'I'm certain she meant it when she said she would get an abortion if I didn't marry her, but as her pregnancy progressed and the baby began to seem more real to her, she genuinely seemed to love it. One thing I could never fault her on was her love for Jason.'

'Maybe she really did love Jonathan . . .?'

'Maybe,' Garrett frowned. 'She never did show him what a bitch she could be.'

'As you said, it's all in the past,' Sarah dismissed briskly. 'It's the future we're concerned with.'

'Oh yes?' A teasing light entered his eyes. 'What future would that be?'

'I'd very much like to be your wife, but I won't ask for marriage if——'

'Won't ask for it!' He hugged her tight. 'I'm going to marry you half a dozen times just so that you know how much I want you for my wife. Starting tonight.'

'Tonight? But——'

'Nevada,' he nodded. 'Then we'll have another wedding in England, then one here, then——'

'Garrett, once would be enough,' she protested happily.

'Once will never be enough with you, my darling,' he told her leeringly.

'Garrett Kingham!' she admonished.

'Yes—Sarah Kingham?' he said softly.

She became suddenly still. 'I'll spend all my life

loving you,' she groaned raggedly.

'I love you more than words can ever say, more than *I* can ever say!'

It was more than enough to build a lifetime of happiness upon.

Sarah smiled glowingly as she heard the commotion outside in the corridor that heralded the arrival of her husband.

The baby hadn't been due for another five weeks, and she had assured Garrett he had plenty of time before the birth to fly over to England for a few days. She would have gone with him, would have enjoyed a couple of days being thoroughly spoilt by her father and Glynis, that kindly lady having become her stepmother a year ago. But she had been feeling so tired recently that they had all thought it would be best if she stayed at home and rested instead.

Eighteen months of marriage had seen her and Garrett's love for each other grow deeper than ever, and she knew he was going to be thrilled at being a father again. Once he had got over the disappointment of missing the birth.

'Sarah!' He burst into the room, laden down with flowers and chocolates he had obviously bought hastily on his way through the airport, the box of chocolates in the shape of a heart, and Valentine's Day wasn't for another two weeks! 'Are you all right? Did you——'

'Calm down, Dad,' the mature youth at his side soothed. 'Can't you see she's fine?'

Because Sarah hadn't been able to go with Garrett she had insisted Jason accompany him; the poor boy had obviously been soothing his father ever since Shelley had telephoned late last night and told him Sarah was in labour!

Garrett came to a halt next to the bed. 'You've had the baby!' He kissed her distractedly.

She looked down ruefully at the flatness of her stomach after months of walking around feeling like a balloon about to burst. 'Yes,' she confirmed patiently.

He swallowed hard, lines of strain visible beside his eyes, his hair tousled, his clothes creased. 'Shelley didn't tell me that when she met us at the airport, and Jonathan didn't say a word outside either . . .'

'Because I wanted to tell you myself,' she explained gently. Shelley and Jonathan had been with her during the long night. 'Jason, get your father a chair, will you?' she prompted indulgently. 'He looks as if he's about to fall down!'

Garrett sat just as the chair was placed beneath him. 'Nothing went wrong, did it?' He was very pale. 'It was so early——'

'Everything went fine,' she smiled reassuringly, including Jason as he stood at the back of the room, a very handsome youth, almost as muscular as Garrett now. 'Join us,' she invited huskily.

'If you're sure . . .?' He still looked uncertain about intruding.

'Don't you want to know if it's a brother or sister you have?' she teased.

He sat in the chair next to his father, both their faces intent.

Sarah drew in a deep breath. 'Garrett, did I ever tell you about Grandmother Harvey, Dad's mother——'

'Darling, this isn't really the time to discuss your family. Unless,' he paled even more, 'your grandmother had something wrong with her, and the baby——'

'There's nothing wrong with the baby, Garrett,' she insisted firmly. 'As I was saying about Grandmother Harvey,' she continued determinedly. 'At the time the family all thought it was just one of those things, after all, it had never happened before, and it hasn't happened since——'

'Sarah, will you tell me whether I have a daughter or another son, and stop frightening the hell out of me!' stormed Garrett tensely.

'I was trying to make this easier for you by——'

'I don't want it made easier, I just want the truth!' His voice rose in his tension.

'All right,' she sighed, smoothing the coverlet beneath her fingers. 'At two-thirty-two this morning our daughter came into the world——'

'A daughter.' Garrett's face glowed with pride. 'Our Diana Louise.'

'Yes.' She met his smile. 'And at two-fifty-six our second daughter was born——'

'*Two* of them?' Garrett gasped disbelievingly, the colour that had flooded back into his face on

being told about his first daughter starting to
recede again.

'Grandmother Harvey was a *twin*,' Jason realised excitedly.

'Er—not exactly,' Sarah replied slowly.

'How not exactly?' Garrett groaned weakly.

She drew in another deep breath. 'At three-ten,
a little quicker this time, our *third* daughter was
born!'

'Triplets!' This time Garrett sagged weakly
back in his chair. 'That is the full count, isn't it?'
The thought suddenly occurred to him. 'There
isn't a son too, is there?'

'No. I thought maybe next time——'

'*Next time?*' He stood up nervily. 'After this I
don't think I could take a *next time*! Why didn't
any of the doctors guess?'

'They did warn me there was a possibility of
twins, but as it was only a possibility I didn't like
to worry you . . .' Sarah trailed off weakly.

'She "didn't like to worry me",' he told his son.
'Oh no, she just decides to give me a heart attack
now! What am I going to do with *three*
daughters?'

'Be proud of them, love them——'

'*Worry* about them,' Garrett tagged on to
Jason's list. '*We* are both going to worry about
them,' he told his son. 'It's a brother's job to
protect his sisters, and if they are anywhere near as
beautiful as their mother——'

'They're much more beautiful than me,' Sarah
put in softly.

'My God, Sarah.' Garrett sat down on the side of the bed, her hands clasped in his. 'Are you all right?'

'Yes.' She laughed softly at the complete panic he had been thrown into.

'Our daughters?'

'Four pounds, four pounds two ounces, and four pounds one ounce respectively,' she reported happily. 'They're a little small at the moment, but they're all perfect, healthy, and beautiful! Your father took one look at them and had to go home to rest!' she recalled with a smile, William Kingham having come to have a grudging respect for her even if they weren't the best of friends.

'Everyone has seen our daughters except Jason and me; can we go and see them?' Garrett had recovered some of his arrogant authority.

'Of course,' she nodded eagerly. 'If you'll just wheel me down we can all go and gaze at the "Kingham Beauties" as they've already been nicknamed!'

She watched Garrett's face as he gazed through the window of the nursery at his three daughters, the pride and love that blazed there the moment he looked at the three identically rounded faces topped by a thatch of midnight-black hair bringing a lump to her throat.

'I think they're going to have green eyes,' she told him in a whisper. 'They're already slightly hazel-blue.'

He swallowed convulsively. 'Maybe next time we *can* have three boys ...'

Sarah laughed softly. 'We have to come up with another two names for our daughters first!'

Garrett's eyes darkened as he looked down at her. 'Are you really all right?'

'Perfect.' She squeezed his hand as they both turned back to gaze at their daughters as they slept.

Maybe next year they *would* try for the three boys . . .

Harlequin Presents

Coming Next Month

1039   THE SHADOW OF MOONLIGHT   Lindsay Armstrong
Meredith Sommerville's marriage was sudden, short and secret from her husband's wealthy family. After his death, the family accept her warmly—all except Evan, the eldest son. He is convinced that Meredith was just an unfaithful fortune hunter!

1040   COUNTRY OF THE HEART   Robyn Donald
Finley was bound to recover from the pneumonia that prompted her vacation. Getting over a man like Blake Caird is another matter. Living together seems impossible—but living apart is infinitely worse. Yet she can't share Blake's island paradise forever!

1041   A REASON FOR MARRIAGE   Penny Jordan
Jamie tells herself she'll never submit to physically becoming Jake's wife. And yet she knows, even as she makes the bitter claim, that she's already given him her heart. Even after six years he still holds it....

1042   KISS OF FIRE   Charlotte Lamb
Impulsively buying race driver Liam Moor's book brings him back into Suzy's life. They share a guilty secret and Liam blames her entirely. He still hates her. She ought to hate him, but underneath is a totally different emotion.

1043   TOO BAD TO BE TRUE   Roberta Leigh
In Leslie's mind, the huge settlement extracted by divorce lawyer Dane Jordan had caused her beloved stepfather's death—and she plans an appropriate revenge. All she has to do is stay out of Dane's arms and keep her heart out of the whole affair....

1044   BURNING INHERITANCE   Anne Mather
Alex has always believed that Isabel's now ended marriage to his cousin was for money, so when she inherits shares in the family company he is delegated to persuade her to sell. Isabel bitterly resents his interference but can't resist the pull of his attraction.

1045   SAVAGE AFFAIR   Margaret Mayo
Tired of fighting off fortune hunters, Rhiannon happily operates an elegant little hotel in the Canary Islands. A mysterious stranger arrives who makes her aware of the passion within her, but when Pasqual's true identity is revealed, her aching love turns to cold hate.

1046   PASSIONATE REVENGE   Sally Wentworth
Seven years has only added to the legacy of bitterness Zara feels at Heath Masterson's rejection. Now she is in a position to extract anything she wants from him. Her head says revenge—but she can't get her heart to agree

Available in January wherever paperback books are sold, or through Harlequin Reader Service:

In the U.S.
901 Fuhrmann Blvd.
P.O. Box 1397
Buffalo, N.Y. 14240-1397

In Canada
P.O. Box 603
Fort Erie, Ontario
L2A 5X3

"GIVE YOUR HEART TO HARLEQUIN" SWEEPSTAKES
OFFICIAL RULES
NO PURCHASE NECESSARY TO ENTER OR RECEIVE A PRIZE

1. To enter and join the Preview Service, scratch off the concealment device on all game tickets. This will reveal the values for each Sweepstakes entry number, the number of free books you will receive, and your free bonus gift as part of our Preview Service. If you do not wish to take advantage of our Preview Service, only scratch off the concealment device on game tickets 1-3. To enter, return your entire sheet of tickets.

2. Either way your Sweepstakes numbers will be compared against the list of winning numbers generated at random by computer. In the event that all prizes are not claimed, random drawings will be held from all entries received from all presentations to award all unclaimed prizes. All cash prizes are payable in U.S. funds. This is in addition to any free, surprise or mystery gifts that might be offered. Versions of this Sweepstakes with different prizes may appear in other mailings or at retail outlets by Torstar Ltd. and its affiliates. This presentation offers the following prizes:

(1)	*Grand Prize	$1,000,000 Annuity
(1)	First Prize	$25,000
(2)	Second Prize	$10,000
(5)	Third Prize	$5,000
(10)	Fourth Prize	$1,000
(2,000)	Fifth Prize	$10

. . . *This presentation contains a Grand Prize offering of a $1,000,000 annuity. Winner may elect to receive $25,000 a year for life up to $1,000,000 or $250,000 in one cash payment. Winners selected will receive the prizes offered in the Sweepstakes promotion they receive.

Entrants may cancel Preview Service at any time without cost or obligation (see details in the center insert card).

3. This promotion is being conducted under the supervision of Marden-Kane, an independent judging organization. By entering the Sweepstakes, each entrant accepts and agrees to be bound by these rules and the decisions of the judges which shall be final and binding. Odds of winning in the random drawing are dependent upon the total number of entries received. Taxes, if any, are the sole responsibility of the winners. Prizes are non-transferable. All entries must be received by March 31, 1988. The drawing will take place on April 30, 1988 at the offices of Marden-Kane, Lake Success, New York.

4. This offer is open to residents of the U.S., Great Britain and Canada, 18 years or older except employees of Torstar Ltd., its affiliates, subsidiaries, Marden-Kane and all other agencies and persons connected with conducting this Sweepstakes. All Federal, State and local laws apply. Void wherever prohibited or restricted by law.

5. Winners will be notified by mail and may be required to execute an affidavit of eligibility and release which must be returned within 14 days after notification. Canadian winners will be required to answer a skill testing question. Winners consent to the use of their name, photograph and/or likeness for advertising and publicity in conjunction with this and similar promotions without additional compensation. One prize per family or household.

6. For a list of our most current prize winners, send a stamped, self-addressed envelope to: WINNERS LIST c/o MARDEN-KANE, P.O. BOX 701, SAYREVILLE, N.J. 08872.

A soaring novel of passion and destiny
as magnificent as the mighty redwoods.

REDWOOD EMPIRE

A.E. MAXWELL

He could offer her the priceless gift of security but could not erase the
sweet agony of desire that ruled her days and tormented her nights.

**For the millions who can't read
Give the Gift of Literacy**

One out of five adults in North America
cannot read or write well enough
to fill out a job application
or understand the directions on a bottle of medicine.

**You can change all this by joining the fight
against illiteracy.**

For more information write to:
Contact, Box 81826, Lincoln, Neb. 68501
In the United States, call toll free: 1-800-228-8813

**The only degree you need
is a degree of caring**

"This ad made possible with the cooperation of the Coalition for Literacy and the Ad Council."
Give the Gift of Literacy Campaign is a project of the book and periodical industry,
in partnership with Telephone Pioneers of America.

Six exciting series for you every month... from Harlequin

Harlequin Romance·
The series that started it all

Tender, captivating and heartwarming...
love stories that sweep you off to faraway places
and delight you with the magic of love.

◆

Harlequin Presents·
Powerful contemporary love stories...as individual as the women who read them

The No. 1 romance series...
exciting love stories for you, the woman of today...
a rare blend of passion and dramatic realism.

◆

Harlequin Superromance®
It's more than romance... it's Harlequin Superromance

A sophisticated, contemporary romance-fiction
series, providing you with a longer,
more involving read...a richer mix of complex plots,
realism and adventure.

Harlequin
American Romance™
Harlequin celebrates the
American woman...

...by offering you romance stories written
about American women, by American women
for American women. This series offers you
contemporary romances uniquely North American
in flavor and appeal.

◆

Harlequin Temptation
Passionate stories for
today's woman

An exciting series of sensual, mature stories of
love...dilemmas, choices, resolutions...
all contemporary issues dealt with in a true-to-life
fashion by some of your favorite authors.

◆

Harlequin Intrigue
Because romance can be quite
an adventure

Harlequin Intrigue, an innovative series that
blends the romance you expect...
with the unexpected. Each story has an added
element of intrigue that provides a new twist to
the Harlequin tradition of romance excellence.

Harlequin Books·

PROD-A-2